True As True Can Be

True As True Can Be

a novel

Thorpe Moeckel

GREEN WRITERS PRESS *Brattleboro, Vermont*

Printed in the United States

10 9 8 7 6 5 4 3 2 1

Green Writers Press is a Vermont-based publisher whose mission is to spread a message of hope and renewal through the words and images we publish. Throughout we will adhere to our commitment to preserving and protecting the natural resources of the earth. To that end, a percentage of our proceeds will be donated to environmental activist groups and social justice organizations. Green Writers Press gratefully acknowledges support from individual donors, friends, and readers to help support the environment and our publishing initiative.

GReen
wrITers
press

Giving Voice to Writers & Artists Who Will Make the World a Better Place
Green Writers Press | Brattleboro, Vermont
www.greenwriterspress.com

ISBN: 978-1-9505840-4-8

COVER & FRONTISPIECE ART BY DONALD SAAF

Visit the Clark Gallery for more information:
www.clarkgallery.com/artists/donald-saaf

THE PAPER USED IN THIS PUBLICATION IS PRODUCED BY MILLS COMMITTED
TO RESPONSIBLE AND SUSTAINABLE FORESTRY PRACTICES.

True As True Can Be

1

From the bridge where she stood, the creek sounded like laughter, and as Lucinda Mae listened to it, she thought of her unexpected fits of giggling that school year. She knew the creek wasn't to blame, but she couldn't figure out why in the middle of lessons, she'd get a funny feeling and just start giggling. She was a happy kid, and normally when she laughed, there was a reason. Her laughter at school was very strange. It was a problem, too. Miss Cartmill had sent her to the hall six times now for disrespect. She claimed that Lucinda Mae's parents would be called to the office if it happened again.

It was a cold morning. Lucinda Mae adjusted her hat, pulled it further down over her ears by bunching her hair—redder than any third grader's hair at Laurel Fork Elementary—up under that yellow wool hat. Beneath her coat, she wore a yellow flannel dress, long-sleeved, that covered her knees. Lucinda Mae was the only student at the school, maybe in the whole state, who wore yellow dresses every day of the year. Yellow was her favorite color. She felt that wearing the dresses, handmade by her mother of different yellow fabrics—corduroy, gingham, rayon, velour—brought her good luck.

That she would need more than luck over the next few days was far from Lucinda Mae's mind. She stood as she always did on her family's oak plank driveway bridge, waiting for the school bus and watching the creek. How the water changed shapes as it ran up against and between the rocks both soothed and energized her. It was late December, 1979, the year nearing its end in a colder than usual way. Ice had been forming for days, and where it blanketed the rocks in the stream's bed, Lucinda Mae saw the water and the milky winter light sparkling in such a way that she knew her teacher, Miss Cartmill, would have called saucy.

Miss Cartmill came from a city. Lucinda Mae heard that every few years teachers from big cities came to work at the school. Lucinda Mae lived in the remote, upstate region of South Carolina called the Gorges, and Laurel Fork Elementary was named, like the local church, for the big stream by the biggest road. Laurel Fork was almost a river, and Painter Creek entered it only a couple of miles from where she now stood. Rumor had it, these teachers were paid extra to work in the Gorges, where few outsiders wanted to live and few insiders stayed once they were old enough to leave. It was no rumor that the teachers who worked at Laurel Fork Elementary rarely lasted more than one year, and Lucinda Mae felt that Miss Cartmill would be ready to go even sooner if she had the chance. Few in the community appeared to trust her, but for no clear reason that Lucinda Mae could understand, except that she was different. Her teacher spoke strangely and kept to herself. Lucinda Mae had also noticed how much her teacher liked to read. She was always reading while the class worked on their lessons. She was also very skinny and pale, which led people to spread other rumors about her private life.

Miss Cartmill wore flare-legged pantsuits to work—city clothes, as many students called them when she wasn't listening. And standing there, skinny as a praying mantis in those city clothes, Miss Cartmill regularly called the things Lucinda Mae said and did saucy. It was strange, but whenever her teacher said the word, Lucinda Mae felt as though many little songbirds were flying in her belly. It was a weird feeling. It kind of tickled. It kind of made her nervous, too. She didn't understand the feeling. Mostly, Lucinda Mae tried not to worry about it, but sometimes she worried about it.

Lucinda Mae was excited and nervous today because she had a story for show and tell, a story based on a photo that her grandmother had shown her over the weekend. It was a true story. One of the rules for show and tell was that all the stories had to be true. Her grandmother, who Lucinda Mae called Mimi, had given her an old black and white photograph that proved the story was true.

As the bus rolled to a noisy stop on the gravel beside the bridge, Lucinda Mae reminded herself that her Mimi's photo was pressed between the pages of her math book. She didn't want to misplace it for show and tell and not have the picture. Lucinda Mae could be forgetful. Just the other day, Miss Cartmill had said, "Being saucy and being forgetful go hand in hand."

Lucinda Mae made her way to an open seat next to her friend, Jean Underwood. Jean lived on up the creek, beyond Old Man Speed's rundown cabin. These girls lived in what some might call a rough holler, but to Lucinda Mae and Jean there were all kinds of wonders and nourishment in the steep, old mountains, in the shadows and wind and plants, in the sound of barking dogs and screeching hawks, and even in the hunters' guns booming in the distance.

"Guess what," Jean said. Jean was wearing jeans. She always wore jeans, blue ones like her eyes. The hood of a red, zippered sweatshirt spilled from the collar of her winter coat. The bus was rolling again.

Lucinda Mae heard flowers in Jean's voice, and in the quiet that followed her two-word question, she sensed that those flowers, yellow flowers, were pushing up through some old, dirty snow. "It's the last day of school before winter break?" she guessed.

"No!" Jean said. "I mean yes, that's true, but guess what . . . Mr. Speed was riding a turtle in his backyard yesterday. My brother Arlen said he saw him. He was sitting on the shell. A big turtle, and Mr. Speed's eyes were closed, my brother said, and he was being taken around the yard, around all the junk and trash just as slow as slow can be."

"Wow," Lucinda Mae said. She liked that Mr. Speed was always doing weird things. She had heard that he ate turtles. That all he ate was stuff from the creek and from the yard. He didn't garden or have a wife that gardened, so he ate weeds. "I heard he eats his weeds like a salad," Lucinda Mae said. She was excited. She liked to talk about Mr. Speed. Joe Speed was his full name—it was written on the old mailbox that had fallen long ago. He was very private. You could make up all kinds of stuff about him and it might be true. "I heard he doesn't even need a lawnmower he eats so much grass and weeds. I heard he likes worms too, and that he likes slugs and bark and fat black ants."

"Maybe," Jean said, "but I think he eats something grosser than that."

"I heard he doesn't have a stove," Lucinda Mae continued. "I heard he has a hole in his floor and he makes a fire there and cooks on it like he was camping."

"Arlen says that he has about a hundred turtles living in his house and he just eats turtle soup. That's about as gross as gross can be."

The girls were giggling pretty heavily now. Lucinda Mae, who was getting warm, pulled the yellow hat off her head and her red, curly hair exploded. She touched it and felt as if some small and very furry animal was using her head for a roost. "I heard he uses the turtle shells for bowls," Lucinda Mae said.

"Arlen says Mr. Speed is a hundred and four years old. He says he's known these hills since they were volcanoes."

"Volcanoes!" Lucinda Mae shrieked. She was laughing so hard now that her whole body shook, but she managed to say, spitting a little as she spoke, "That's about as much of a lie as can be. Arlen's putting you on."

"I hope so," Jean snorted. Both girls were quaking with laughter. They didn't even notice the other kids on the bus shooting them glances. "I sure hope so," Jean continued.

❧ ❧

After her bus ride with Jean, Lucinda Mae set her mind on school and did well on her morning math and spelling lessons. She glanced from her desk now and then at her teacher. Miss Cartmill looked tired again. She always looked tired. She had dark bags under her pretty green eyes, and she moved like she'd been digging for hours in hard ground. Her jawline and chin seemed even more narrow. Even her eyebrows, normally dark and full like her hair, seemed like they'd diminished. And her small ears were so red that Lucinda Mae thought she could feel the heat coming from them. The girl wondered if she was having trouble sleeping. And maybe having trouble eating, too. The lady was so skinny. Her arms were like sticks.

There was an hour before lunch period. Just as Lucinda Mae reached into her desk where she'd stashed her Mimi's photograph, she heard Miss Cartmill announce in that accent of hers, sharp, like how trees look in winter instead of summer, "It's time for show and tell. Who would like to go first?"

The photo slipped and Lucinda Mae lifted her hand up for balance while with the other hand she reached for the old black-and-white that lay face down on the floor.

"Lucinda Mae," Miss Cartmill said. "Good of you to volunteer. Come on up."

Lucinda Mae growled to herself. She didn't want to go first. She carried the photo to the front of the class. She looked out at her classmates in their desks and remembered the way the water in Painter Creek moved over the rocks and through the ice. She heard the water's laughter, but she didn't feel any urge to giggle herself, which was a relief. She felt only a bit nervous as she began to speak:

"This is a story that my grandmother told me. It is a true story about Christmas and a one-eyed lady in a red dress and her carriage. You probably won't believe that it's true, but I'll pass around a picture at the end to show you it is.

"Back a while ago when my grandmother was a girl, she said they were having a real warm winter and it was getting to be Christmastime and still they hadn't had a frost and there were still ticks being pulled from the dogs and even flies were still a problem. It was too warm to hang meat and things felt pretty wrong and people were nervous and stuff. My Mimi—that's my grandmother—well, my Mimi's uncle, Uncle Roy, came to visit for Christmas and brought with him a camera. Cameras were pretty new still and only took pictures in black and white. Uncle Roy brought his camera back from the war. He really liked my Mimi and gave her lessons on how to use it and even let her take it out when he wasn't around. I never knew this man, but my Mimi says he was a little different on account of the war and liked to spend a lot of time alone in the woods looking at animals and plants and taking pictures of them.

"On this year, on the day before Christmas Eve, Uncle Roy went out carousing in the hills and forgot he'd left the camera with Mimi. When it got late on Christmas Eve and he hadn't come home, the family went out looking for him. Like I said, it was a real warm winter. They lived way back Painter Creek, at the top of the valley, and my Mimi's daddy figured Uncle Roy had gone out to look after animals and might be hurt. Mimi was fifteen then and knew the woods up there real good. They told her to go up a side branch, one of those that drops off the big side of Painter Mountain.

Well, she did, she went, and though she was supposed to leave her uncle's camera at home, she snuck it up the mountain with her. The moon was big, my Mimi said, and the branch was steep, and at the top, way up there where it seems like Painter Mountain is about to scrape the sun and bust your lungs, like it's mad at you for climbing it, up there where things level out, there weren't a lot of trees on account of a fire on the mountain the summer prior. Well, she was up there just sweating and stuff in the winter heat and hollering for her Uncle Roy when she comes upon the darnedest thing. It was a one-eyed lady in a red dress."

"Like I have fourteen bellybuttons," Lucinda Mae heard someone mutter from the back of the classroom. There were other noises, sneers and snickers, even after Miss Cartmill raised her bony hand to shush them.

Lucinda Mae continued despite the commotion. It felt to her like the story was telling itself. "Mimi, she's off to the side and the one-eyed lady doesn't see her so she stays put and is real quiet and stuff, and a little nervous, just watching. The lady is fiddling with a mess of animals and a big carriage and leather straps for a harness. My Mimi saw she was a dark-haired lady and beaded with sweat and wearing that thick, red work dress, and that she was tying off a bunch of big old deer-like critters. Just talking to them sure and comfortable like you talk to your friend on the bus. At the same time, off to the side there's standing a wild turkey, a red fox, a painter—I mean panther—an osprey, a whitetail deer, and a brook trout. I still don't know how a brook trout can be standing but just you wait till you see the picture."

"I'm waiting," the kid Morris Deacon said with a sneer.

"Me, too," someone else snorted. Lucinda Mae felt a pang of embarrassment, a brief but sharp one, and then she looked at Jean. Jean was giving Morris a look that could melt steel. Lucinda Mae smiled. Seeing Jean quieted her fluster. Lucinda Mae liked this story and how telling it felt as if she was wading in the swimming hole at Painter Creek on a hot summer day. And Morris Deacon, she thought with a grin, he was like a gnat, funny and easily ignored. She glanced at a map on the wall at the back of the room and kept on.

"So my Mimi's watching real quiet and stuff, but her legs are stiff and hurting from standing so still after such a long walk up the mountain, so she steps and comes down on a twig. That breaks, and the lady with the red dress sees the ears on the critters get tense and turn, and she looks and sees my Mimi there, standing alone, sweating in the moonlight on that bald, burnt place on the mountain.

'Are you lost?' she says.

'No, ma'am,' my Mimi says.

'What are you doing way up here?' the lady asks.

'I'm looking for my Uncle Roy,' she says. And then my Mimi asks, and she's still nervous, 'What are you doing? Are you lost? Who are you?'

'I'm not lost. I'm fixing a problem,' the one-eyed lady says. 'And your uncle was just here, not long ago.'

'What's your problem?' my Mimi wonders.

'It's too warm for my reindeer. They're cold weather animals. Even up high in the air, it's too warm this year. They're going to get hurt and maybe fall and take me with them,' the lady said. Now she paused to wipe her forehead with a bandanna that was only slightly redder than her flushed, full cheeks, and then continued. "I'm planning to tie them off here and leave them until the cold weather comes. But meanwhile I have to get these presents delivered, so with the help of your uncle and another young man named Speed, I've assembled a new crew to pull my carriage. They're going to be the perfect carriage-pullers for this kind of weather. I had to diversify, I mean."

'What's diversify mean?' says my Mimi.

'Diversify,' the lady says. 'It means having a good mix. It means having all your bases covered in case of this or that.'

Well, my Mimi understands this and she goes on watching as the lady does her work, tying off the reindeer and hitching the other animals to the carriage. Mimi said she hitched the team like so: wild turkey and fox up front, and behind them the brook trout and panther, and the deer and the osprey closest to the carriage.

'Young woman, I wonder if you'd do me a favor,' the one-eyed lady says then to my Mimi. 'It's a lot to ask, but would you come up here and feed and water my reindeer?' she says. 'Until it gets cold enough, I mean. Cold enough for me to come back.'

Well, to not take up too much of you all's time, my Mimi says she'll do that favor. And then she asks if she can take a photograph of the one-eyed lady and the animals, and the lady says sure. So Mimi takes a picture of them taking off, the reindeer in their corral and the carriage coming off the bald and burnt ground, being pulled by the wild turkey, the red fox, the osprey, the whitetail deer, and the brook trout and the panther. Here you go, here's my Mimi's picture—see for yourself—but please be real careful with it."

She was about to hand the picture to the boy Tommy Grimes who always sat in the front row, but Miss Cartmill scurried up and snatched it away. The classroom buzzed. Her story, it was clear, had not rung true. But Lucinda Mae knew her story was true, she just knew it was, and yet now she felt—like termites, she thought, like little teeth—the beginnings of doubt. She was nervous as Miss Cartmill stood there skinny and stern as ever in her dark-brown polyester pantsuit. Lucinda Mae could still in her mind see the photo of the fire-damaged mountain, the one-eyed lady in the carriage, the odd assortment of animals hitched to the carriage, the reindeer in the corral.

The teacher turned back to Lucinda Mae now. "Santa, in Spanish, means a female saint," she said after a bit, but she spoke more to herself than the class.

Lucinda Mae felt a laugh rise in her throat. There was nothing funny. She snorted as she held it down, and felt nervous and angry and sad all at once. She bit her tongue. She could have easily started crying. Miss Cartmill, meanwhile, stood there, hands on her pencily hips.

After a long minute, Miss Cartmill looked down at her from the picture. "You're some storyteller, Lucinda Mae," she said, and as her teacher paused again, took a long breath, Lucinda Mae wondered if Miss Cartmill saying "You're some storyteller" was a bad thing or a good thing, and, if it was a good thing, she wanted to know if it was just a teacher being kind or a teacher being true. "Now be careful with this," Miss Cartmill said as she handed the photo to Tommy Grimes in the front row.

2

The next morning, Lucinda Mae woke to two inches of fresh snow. She felt her yellow cotton nightgown clinging to her; there was static electricity, as there often is in winter, and she felt it making her hair go every which way. Through the one window, brightness filled her small bedroom, and as she stared at it, it warmed her insides.

It was the first day of winter break from school. After doing her chicken chores and eating breakfast, Lucinda Mae helped her mother in the house. She stripped the beds, scrubbed the bathtub, changed her brother's diaper, and made four crusts to be frozen for holiday pies. Lucinda Mae felt good. She felt in touch with what her father and mother often called "her gift for getting it done."

Now her mother had gone to put her baby brother down for a nap. Lucinda Mae was washing up the last mixing bowl and thinking about frying some venison bologna for lunch when she heard someone at the door. Lucinda Mae knew from the pattern of the knocking that it was Jean from up the hollow.

"Lucinda's not home," Lucinda Mae said in her deepest voice. She knew that Jean knew that Mr. Coggins left at five thirty each morning except Sunday for his job at the post office, but she tried to sound like her father anyway.

"Quit it!" Jean yelled in response. Lucinda Mae grinned and opened the door then. She yanked it hard, all that pale winter light pouring through, and ran back to the sink as if to make it seem the wind had opened the door.

"That trick's older than these hills," Jean said. "But guess what?" she went on as she sat up on one of the stools by the chopping block. Lucinda Mae felt a calm giddiness come over her as she glanced at her friend, her short, thick, strong figure. Jean looked fidgety as usual, but in that excited more than nervous way. She saw that Jean's mother had recently trimmed her straight black hair in short bangs and tapered it to shoulder length in the back. Something about Jean's hair, and Lucinda Mae couldn't put her finger on it, reminded her that Jean was a year and a month older than her.

"What?" Lucinda Mae began, pausing as she felt a smirk coming on. "I don't know, is Miss Cartmill spending Christmas with you?"

"No way," Jean said, scrunching her nose like she'd eaten an unripe persimmon. "My parents say if she's teaching again next year, they'll school me at home or something."

"I think Miss Cartmill's not well," Lucinda Mae said. "She seems so tired."

"She's wasting away," Jean said. "And you know what? I overheard a guy at the grocery say that he thinks she's working for the government. Like she's a spy. Like she's checking up on Laurel Fork for the president and stuff. But guess, go on, you stopped guessing. I mean, today's the *day*. You've got to guess."

"The day for what?"

"That's what you're guessing!" Jean said. She really was excited. Lucinda Mae wondered why Jean's parents let her drink coffee. She was only ten.

"It's the day school's out," Lucinda Mac said.

"Yes," Jean said, "but it's also the day that we see what Old Man Speed is really doing in that rundown place of his." Jean was off the stool, wiggling a little in her jeans and watching Lucinda Mae scrub the mixing bowl. "Your wash water is as dirty as dirty can be. I'd change that water if I was you."

Lucinda Mae wiped the ceramic bowl a few more wipes. And then she rinsed and inspected it. The bowl looked clean. It was one of those bowls with a pleasing shape. It was blue on the outside and pearly white in the mouth. Pouring places curved out opposite one another; they reminded Lucinda Mae of soccer goals, and for a moment she imagined miniature people playing soccer in the bowl, running up and down as well as across the flatter portion of the bowl's bottom. Lucinda Mae liked playing soccer during recess at school. "The water's fine," she said to Jean at last, "and you know what? It's a fine day to spy on Mr. Speed."

"Well, how's this for fine?" Jean said. "Arlen says Old Man Speed never locks his doors or even his windows."

"Neither do we," said Lucinda Mae. She was finished with the mixing bowl. The bowl now stood on its edge on the drying rack. Lucinda Mae wiped her hands on a dish cloth. "Who in Painter Hollow locks their doors? Everybody thinks we're all crazy in Painter Hollow. Nobody's going to mess with us."

"When are you going to be ready?" Jean asked Lucinda Mae. Lucinda Mae was reminded that this was a pattern for them. She was always finishing some chore while Jean was anxious to get going. Maybe, Lucinda Mae thought, it was the difference between being a youngest child, as Jean was, and being the oldest, as she was.

"I'll be ready," Lucinda Mae said, "before you can lick the scales off of Mr. Speed's favorite turtle."

"That's gross," Jean said with glee.

"Cinda," Jean continued after a pause. Lucinda Mae was down under the sink, looking for a new sponge. She didn't notice how Jean's voice had changed suddenly, grown serious. "Are you nervous about spying on Old Man Speed?"

"I'm excited about it," Lucinda Mae said as she emerged from the dark cabinet. Now she was down on the kitchen floor, on her knees, red sponge in her left hand. "Excited and nervous both. You know that story I told at school about the one-eyed lady? It's pretty neat that Speed was there."

"Yes," Jean said. "I wonder about that story, your Mimi. It's really weird. But you know what's not hard to believe?" Jean paused. "That we don't have to go to school today! It's winter break!"

"Yes, that's good, no bus, no school stuff at all," Lucinda Mae added. "And we've been talking about spying on Speed since we were six!" She stood now and cut the sponge in half with kitchen shears. Her mother never saw the need for such a large sponge. She was a thrifty woman.

"True," Jean said. "But I kind of wish we'd done it back then, when we didn't know any better."

"Know any better about what?" Lucinda Mae asked.

"Like how people can be about trespassers, how they can treat them if they catch them."

"How's that?"

"I don't know," Jean said. "But a lot of things come to mind, none of them very nice."

⤙⤚

The snow was melting off the roofs of the house and the outbuildings when the girls stepped outside, both of them warm though a little slow-moving with a thick slice of fried venison bologna in each of their bellies. Their plan, decided while fixing some lunch, was to approach Mr. Speed's place by way of the thick growth along the creek.

So they went, and now a deer trail became their path. It was simple but tense walking, and not far from Speed's—who lived less than a mile upstream—they were frightened to discover boot prints in the snow where they stepped, boot prints and some other, smaller prints next to them.

"Whose feet are these?" Jean wondered in a hushed tone.

"Maybe it was Arlen," Lucinda Mae whispered. "He's always out poking around."

"These prints are too big for him," Jean said.

"He's twelve now," Lucinda Mae said. "He's pretty tall."

"But these aren't my brother's feet," Jean said. "I know his feet. He paid me a nickel for every splinter I tweezered from them last summer after he danced barefoot on Dad's lumber pile."

"What was he dancing on that rough lumber pile for?" Lucinda Mae snickered, but she quickly checked her volume.

"Uncle Larry was practicing the mandolin out by the springhouse," Jean said. "I guess Arlen liked the music a lot. You know how Arlen is, those sudden bursts he has."

They were nearing Speed's place. They were moving more slowly. An old wooden leg stood in the yard just like it always did, but it felt to Lucinda Mae even more creepy to see it with a dollop of snow at the top. Jean, who walked past his house to catch the school bus, had often wondered aloud to her whether his new wooden leg was different than this one, like maybe was it metal now instead of wood.

"How many nickels did you get?" Lucinda Mae asked.

"Fifty five cents," Jean whispered. She was crouched down, studying Speed's yard.

"Why don't we circle around by that outhouse?" Lucinda Mae suggested.

"Okay," Jean said. There was a hush of nervous excitement in her voice, but she followed anyway. It wasn't the first time she'd followed Lucinda Mae somewhere scary. It wouldn't be the last.

They scurried, bent at the waist, to the far side of the outhouse. There was a wood canoe on the ground, leaning against the back wall. It was old, heavy-looking, perhaps even carved from a log. Jean waited as Lucinda Mae peered around the corner.

"I don't see anyone in the windows," Lucinda Mae said.

"No turtles or anything?" Jean wondered.

"Nothing." There was a shovel resting against the tar paper wall of the outhouse, and Jean, without meaning to knock it over, knocked it over.

"Leave it!" Lucinda Mae said. The hairs on the back of her neck felt like a caterpillar, a busy one. She took several deep breaths. "I'm going to get up under that window by the boxwood and see if there's anything going on in there."

"What should I do?" Jean asked, her words fast with fear.

"Keep me covered," Lucinda Mae said. "Watch my back."

"Let's just go home," Jean said.

Lucinda Mae looked at her friend, and when their eyes met it was like a ruckus of hens all through her body, like someone had just showed up with feed after forgetting for a day or two. Lucinda Mae looked at the house and then back at Jean, and then she ran to the window.

Lucinda Mae felt a deep awareness. There were birds eating bread parts out the back door. They were fluttering down from and back up to an old elm from which stray bits of rope and wire dangled. Beyond the tree stood an old stump turned on edge, its heartwood variously sliced as if from a hatchet being thrown into it.

Lucinda Mae knelt under the window sill, felt the snow cold and wet against the knees of her tights. She shifted to a squat and looked back at Jean, whose round, eager face peeped from around the outhouse. With a head motion only a good friend could understand, she asked Jean if she saw any movement in the window. Jean shook her head. The birds sounded nervous now. Fewer birds came to the bread, but a whole ruckus of them fluttered about the elm. They had slick coloring and hooked beaks and pretty voices. Lucinda Mae felt their song behind her eyelids. She peeked over the sill now, her eyes adjusting to the light inside the house.

The house's interior appeared simple and tidy, much nicer than it looked from the outside. It wasn't a large place; Lucinda Mae could see through to the kitchen, which was at the rear. The fireplace, she saw, opened through to the front room, providing heat to both parts of the house. For some reason it scared her how neat everything looked.

The back door stood beyond a small table. Many jars, pints and quarts and half gallons, lined the shelves. They appeared to be filled with dried leaves, faded greens and browns. A stack of canes leaned against the corner by a pantry with a curtain pulled over it.

There was nothing on the white walls—no clock, no pictures, nothing.

Lucinda Mae scrambled back to where Jean kept watch from the outhouse. The birds in the elm reminded her of her heart, the way it was beating now. She looked at Jean and saw her friend's shoulders were very tense. "Are you mad at me for running over there?" she asked.

"A little, but I forgive you," Jean said. "What did you see?"

"A kitchen! It was tidy, too tidy," Lucinda Mae said. "Everything was quiet. Too quiet. I didn't feel any footsteps or hear a thing."

"Maybe he's still asleep?" Jean said.

"I doubt it," Lucinda Mae said, nodding with her head towards the footprints in the snow. She understood now those odd divots beside each right footprint. Speed walked with a cane. She also knew right then that she and Jean's footprints would give them away. She wondered if the snow might melt by evening. The day was warming, but the days were short now. And the warmth was moist, and the wind, out of the southwest, had a certain chill to it. It was strange weather, hard to predict.

༄ ༄

Lucinda Mae and Jean entered through the front door. It wasn't locked because there wasn't a lock on it.

Lucinda Mae had smelled wood smoke outside, so she wasn't surprised to find glowing embers in the stone hearth. The glow stared like eyes, mean ones. She tried not to look at the fire. A mount of gobbler feathers stood above the mantle. It looked made for that place. Lucinda Mae felt strange, like she was floating. She looked at Jean, who appeared still willing to abandon their mission, to go home for more bologna, maybe a mug of hot cocoa with some playing in the snow afterwards. It looked like she'd even help with chores. Anything. But Lucinda Mae knew her friend, knew how reliable she was, as if Jean's doubts gave her strength, staying power.

"Do you think he's here?" Jean asked Lucinda Mae.

Lucinda Mae felt herself pause for a moment, and then she smiled.

"Anybody home?" she asked out loud. Jean nearly choked at the sound.

There was no reply. Lucinda Mae asked again, this time in an ever sweeter tone. Again there was no reply. The girls looked at one another, but what passed between them in that look this time was mysterious. Lucinda Mae turned. She was drawn to a whole mess of things on the table and on the floor at the north wall, and she approached it.

Jean, meanwhile, stood near the front door and watched the windows in case somebody approached. Being the lookout suited her. She had better vision than Lucinda Mae; in their explorations, she spotted hawks and squirrels and salamanders with much more frequency. And Jean was never "it" very long in games of hide and seek.

On a table there lay open a large book, the oversized pages busy with inkwork, crisp handwriting. There were sketches in the margins and sometimes in the center of the page, sketches of plants and berries and of the human body and animal bodies, too. They were intricate with detail, and Lucinda Mae felt a little squirmy as she looked at them. The book had a medical purpose, Lucinda Mae decided after flipping through the thick pages, but there were also maps in it. The maps were hand-drawn. One of the maps, Lucinda Mae could tell, was of Painter Mountain. Her dad and mom were proud of her for how well she'd learned to read maps, and looking now at the old-fashioned map, she saw how accurate it was. She could even tell where her house was, and she saw, too, the spot where they were right now. What she noticed most of all was how big and broad Painter Mountain was, with all its ridges and hollows.

Lucinda Mae was scared and also fascinated by the book but even more by all the other items. It was a strange, creepy collection. There were rabbit pelts stretched on bent clothes hangers. There were probably a dozen mortar and pestles of all shapes and sizes, and with different powdery residue in each. Her mother used a stone mortar and pestle for mixing spices, and Lucinda Mae liked to be given that job—something to do with the feel of stone on stone, something even older than old-fashioned. On the shelves behind the table there were jars of rocks, jars of snakeskins, satchels of nuts, a row of knives. Notebooks in stacks, some of them old, the pages yellowing. An ancient baseball mitt. A huge box of antlers—deer, goat, sheep, even a moose. And in a basket was a pile of at least five turtle shells, each from a different kind of turtle. Lucinda Mae recognized the common box turtle as well as the mud turtle. Something about all these things made Lucinda Mae very glad they'd chosen to enter Old Man Speed's home, but at the same time she felt more nervous than ever. Her mind raced. She knew it was wrong to be here, but she also knew that doing wrong could sometimes lead to good, and this pile of things gave her a hunch that if something good came out of their adventure today, it might be very good. Or else it might be very bad.

"Cinda," Jean said. Her voice was tense, almost angry. "Did you see all these oil lamps?"

"I hadn't noticed," Lucinda Mae said.

"He doesn't have electric lights," Jean said. "I don't see a one."

"Right," Lucinda Mae said, looking around. "And I didn't see an oven in the kitchen earlier."

"Let's check," Jean said, but she stood still so Lucinda Mae might lead the way.

They were right about the stove. They discovered an assortment of skillets hanging from cut nails over the fireplace, but no stove, not even a wood cookstove. A Dutch oven stood by the iron poker and a shovel and brush, and Lucinda Mae removed its lid to reveal a stew, its fats not yet congealed, lots of bones poking this way and that. Lucinda Mae felt herself breathing fast and shallow as Jean pointed to a pile of coals that must have been the heat source for Speed's breakfast, the way they were flattened and stained from juices boiling over. An iron tea kettle hung by its handle on the iron arm of a post. When Lucinda Mae pushed it, the arm swiveled closer to the fire. She pulled it back to its original position.

"Oh gosh," Jean gasped.

"What?" Lucinda Mae said quickly, but as she turned she saw. There was a collection of knives on the kitchen table, as well as stones for sharpening them. She counted nine different knives. Not all of them were long. They looked sharp. One of them, its blade thin from so much sharpening, appeared stained with blood.

"Let's get out of here," Jean said. She was already moving towards the door.

Lucinda Mae hurried after her friend, but she stopped because she felt like she was leaving something behind. She thought of the map of Painter Mountain. She knew she had to take it. She ran back to the table and ripped that page from the binding, folded it quickly, and slipped it in the pocket of her dress.

Once out of the house, she followed as Jean ran to the road, where it might be safer to travel than in the woods back on the other side of the creek, Speed's side.

"Scary," Jean said as she caught her breath.

Lucinda Mae sighed. Things were happening too quickly. She looked down the road. There was a sound coming from that direction, a sound like a car.

After a minute, the car appeared from around the bend, a strange car.

"Let's hide," Jean said. "Quick!"

The car approached. It moved slowly. It was a small, newish car, and the sun reflected from it with a hurtful brightness. "No," Lucinda Mae said. "This is the road we live on. It's okay."

"I hope so," Jean said, her eyes big, her head shaking like a bug had flown in her ear.

"It's a Pinto," Lucinda Mae said. "My dad thinks they're funny cars."

"Like the bean?" Jean wondered aloud just as the car pulled alongside the girls.

"Well, well, well," said Miss Cartmill through the open window. She was wearing sunglasses, the city kind that made her look like a June bug. Her hair was, as usual, only partly combed. Lucinda Mae registered that her teacher was dressed real wild and pretty, in a tomato-red quilted coat with huge collars and a long skirt with squiggly-patterned colors—blues, yellows, pinks, greens, reds. No brown pantsuit today.

"Hello, Miss Cartmill!" Jean said. Lucinda Mae could hear how her friend was trying too hard to mask her nervousness, but she knew that Jean was on better terms with their teacher than she was, if better meant not being on much of any terms.

"Jean, Lucinda Mae—good to see you," their teacher said. There was a forced sound to her friendliness and she did not remove her sunglasses. Lucinda Mae imagined her tired eyes behind the lenses. Her fingers on the steering wheel reminded Lucinda Mae of worms drying on hot concrete. She didn't wear even one ring. "Out for a walk?" the teacher asked.

"Yes, ma'am," Jean answered too cheerfully. Lucinda Mae nodded in agreement.

"What are you doing up here?" Lucinda Mae asked then, but as soon as she heard the words leave her mouth she wished she could fetch them back.

"On a drive," the teacher said. "Never been up this road before. It's pretty here."

"We live on this road," Jean said.

"That's what I hear," Miss Cartmill said. Her voice sounded like dry leaves. Lucinda Mae wanted to ask if she was sick. "What's that creek called?"

"Painter Creek," Lucinda Mae said. An image of all those knives ran through her head, and then she remembered the table with all the weird things, and then she remembered the voices of her class-mates jeering at her during show and tell. Her heart raced—she felt it in her neck—and she knew a strong and sudden urge to see Speed's house again. She took a deep breath, thought of the map in her pocket, and listened as a dog started barking up the hollow. "Miss Cartmill, are you sick?" Lucinda Mae asked.

There was a strange pause. The air felt heavier, the creeknoise very loud. Lucinda Mae felt a mix of relief and yuckiness, like she'd just swallowed a spoonful of bad tasting medicine. Their teacher looked ahead and then she looked at her hands on the steering wheel. She looked annoyed and also saddened. "I'm doing fine," she answered with a weak smile. "But I must say, you girls look frightened." Miss Cartmill glanced at the mountain then, the dark winter trees against the snow. "It's okay. School's out. Nobody's in trouble. And what a pretty day."

Jean and Lucinda Mae stole a look at one another, and then Lucinda Mae spoke. "We better be getting on home, Miss Cartmill. And, also, I really love your skirt."

"Me too," the lady said. "And thank you. This skirt is very special to me. Glad to see you in yellow even when school's out, Lucinda Mae," she added with a weak smile.

The girls started again down the road. They were relieved to hear Miss Cartmill's car drive on beyond them.

"That was weird," Lucinda Mae said after a while. What she wanted to say then was *I wish we could help her*, but instead she muttered something about wondering where their teacher was going.

"Yes, weird," Jean said. She kicked a chunk of gravel. They walked at a faster pace than normal. "You know," she continued, "I heard she might get fired. The parent association thinks she might be better suited for another school district. I heard they really didn't like that book she made us read."

"What book?" Lucinda Mae asked as they neared the bridge that started her driveway.

"The one about the lady and her boat."

"I liked that book," Lucinda Mae said. "That was a great adventure. I mean, sailing around the world all by herself—that lady did some amazing stuff."

"I guess so," Jean said. "I did real bad on the book report. I got a bad grade." They stood for a moment over Painter Creek. Lucinda Mae stared at the water, remembering the book, the story, the ocean, life on a sailboat alone. Jean continued, "And you remember how she was teaching us about pesticides and Rachel What's-her-name, all that environmentalism stuff?"

"I do," Lucinda Mae said. "That was one of the days she fainted."

"They didn't like that either, the parents."

"She's the teacher," Lucinda Mae said after a minute. "They're the parents. And good grades are good to get but they don't have diddly to do with what a good person you are, Jean. You're my best friend forever."

"I don't know," Jean said, smiling a little. "But I could use some more bologna. A glass of milk would be good, too."

"Sure," said Lucinda Mae. She was still staring at the rushing creek, and when she looked up, everything appeared for a moment to be liquid, to be moving. She did not close her eyes.

3

The Coggins' kitchen was warm, bright, and smelled fresh, like clean, busy kitchens do. The girls sat at the table. They had finished their snack. They sipped from glasses of milk. Lucinda Mae's mother had gone for a walk when the girls returned. She'd left Peanut with them. The boy was down for his afternoon nap.

"What if Arlen was wrong?" Lucinda Mae said. Her voice had revved up again. Fright and curiosity had made a nest deep in her mind.

"What if?" Jean said.

"I don't know," Lucinda Mae answered. "Everybody has knives."

"Speed is some kind of crazy hermit," Jean added. "It's clear as can be. And I don't want to go back there."

"But I have a weird feeling," Lucinda Mae countered. "I need to see that place again. There's something going on in there. That pile of things, it feels important. I don't know why."

"Let's do something else," Jean said. "Let's," she paused, "let's go to the vine swing."

"Wait, I almost forgot about this," Lucinda Mae said as she reached into the pocket of her dress.

Jean watched as she opened the page. "You stole that," Jean said as much as asked. "How could you have forgotten that you stole something from Mr. Speed?"

"I borrowed it, and I can be forgetful."

"That's Painter Mountain," Jean said, her finger touching the page.

"Yes," Lucinda Mae said, "but move your hand, please. Something is written on the back of it; I hadn't noticed that before."

Jean moved her hand, and Lucinda Mae flipped over the page. There was writing in the bottom left corner, a list, and she read it aloud:

Carol Cartmill, age 27, female

Complains of: stomach cramps, no appetite, body aches, not sleeping

Since 1976, 3 yrs.

Last doctor visit: Dec. 1978, no clear diagnosis, symptoms worsening.

Lucinda Mae looked at Jean. Jean was shaking her head. She looked just as confused and sad as Lucinda Mae felt. "We need to go back to Speed's," Lucinda Mae said.

"Now?"

"Soon as we possibly can. There might be more clues there about Miss Cartmill and—"

Mrs. Coggins entered the kitchen from the mud-room then, her face flushed with exertion.

"Hi, Mom," Lucinda Mae said with a forced calm. Her mother looked at her quickly, as if trying to read behind her daughter's greeting.

"You girls get enough to eat?" Mrs. Coggins said. She stood at the sink, washing her hands.

"Plenty," Jean said. Mrs. Coggins turned. She smiled. She was a beautiful woman. She had brown hair in a thick braid, broad shouldered with expressive, capable hands and eyes that seemed to smile, too.

"I take it Peanut's still sleeping."

"Yes," Lucinda Mae answered. "A good walk?"

"Good," said her mom as she sat at the table. "But you know who I saw?" The girls looked at one another. The woman did not wait for their answer. "I saw Old Man Speed. And you know who was with him? Who was driving him, headed out Painter Hollow Road, headed to Laurel Fork?" The girls still looked at one another. Their eyes were larger, as if with shared sight.

"Your teacher," Lucinda Mae's mother said. "Miss Cartmill." After a long look at the girls, she continued. "I see you find that as strange as I do."

"Did you all talk?" Jean asked.

"Real briefly," Mrs. Coggins said. "It was mighty odd. I've heard so many things about both of them, that to see them together . . . in that funny car . . . I just don't know."

"Do you like Miss Cartmill?" Jean asked, continuing, "I like your overalls, by the way." Lucinda Mae shot her friend an annoyed glance.

"Oh," Mrs. Coggins started. "I like these overalls, too." Lucinda Mae could tell her mom was fixing her words. "I don't know. I don't really know her. But I hear things, things that I don't like to hear."

"What about Old Man Speed?" Jean continued. She needed to back off, Lucinda Mae thought. Jean went on, "Everybody says he's a nuts old man."

"Sometimes there's truth in gossip," Mrs. Coggins said. "But I don't like to pass judgment." Her tone had changed. "You all just keep your distance from Mr. Speed and everything will be fine. He's grown stranger in his old age." Lucinda Mae stared out the window. She could just make out a sliver of the creek below the pool where she liked to dunk herself in hot months. She thought of the creek and she thought of the times she'd overheard people at church talking about Speed, using words like heathen, plant medicine, strange, and dangerous. Something about an old folks home, a relative around Toccoa. She wondered if the words they'd used were their own or what they had heard and were repeating, trying to sort out. She never understood what her parents thought of him, but she knew there were doubts. Most of the people in and around Laurel Fork seemed funny about Mr. Speed.

"Mama," she said. "We're going up to Jean's for a while. Is that okay?"

"Sure, Cinda," her mother said. Lucinda Mae felt that familiar look, like her mama knew everything she was thinking even before she herself did. But the girl ignored it. "Just be back before dark," Mrs. Coggins added after a moment.

❧ ❧

Lucinda Mae resorted to bribery. She promised Jean half a stick of bologna if she'd go back to Speed's with her. Jean loved venison bologna more than candy, but it wasn't served in her house. So she agreed to one more time.

The girls were on their way. They followed their own tracks through the brushy growth back to Speed's house. There was only the faintest bit of smoke coming from the chimney now. "He's gone," Lucinda Mae said. "With Miss Cartmill. In that fancy car. It's now or never."

"How are you so sure?" Jean asked, but before she finished saying the word, Lucinda Mae had darted for the outhouse.

Jean threw up her arms, but it wasn't long before she followed. "I'll stand watch here. I'm not going back in."

"Come on," Lucinda Mae said. She didn't want to go in alone. She sensed that her bravery was not entirely her own.

"Can we make it fast?" Jean asked.

"Of course."

"But check the window again in case," Jean insisted.

"Okay." Lucinda Mae ran to the window. She saw the same things in the same places. Only the angle of the light and the beat of her heart were different now. She felt that there was something scarier about going in the man's house a second time, but she decided not to examine it. She darted back to Jean.

"Come on, Jean. It's clear. He's not home."

"Cinda Mae, I swear," Jean said as she followed her friend to the door without a lock.

&⸱⸱&

They were back in the house. Lucinda Mae moved with haste. Her mother's warning about Mr. Speed was fresh in her mind. She went directly to the oversized sketchbook, and knelt, and started to flip through the pages again. Nothing of particular interest caught her eye.

Jean had been standing behind her, but now tiptoed around the corner into the kitchen. "Cinda, here quick," she said.

"What."

"Look here."

Lucinda Mae stood. The air in the house felt funny for a moment, and she tried to ignore it. She went around to the kitchen.

"The knives are gone."

"So?" Lucinda Mae said.

"It means he could be home," Jean said. Her voice sounded weak.

"He's not home," Lucinda Mae said.

"Who says I'm not home?" The voice was that of a man. It came from the front room. It might as well have been a gunshot.

Lucinda Mae heard the door shut and then footsteps and then—it could only be—the tap of a cane. She stood straighter as Jean grabbed her hand. She looked at the fireplace like it might tell her what to say.

"Hello," Jean said in a voice both sweeter and more mature somehow than Lucinda Mae had ever heard from her friend. The tone of it sent sparks through her bones, and she could not remember how to breathe.

"Well, I'll be," said the man. It was, no doubt about it, Old Man Speed—tall, dark-haired, gaunt, slightly stooped, but strong, the lines on his face reminding Lucinda Mae of the hatchet marks in the stump out back. A pointy tuft of white hair grew from his chin while the rest of his face was clean-shaven. He wore a leather hat with three guinea fowl feathers on the right side of the band. His jacket was made of some other skin, and in Lucinda Mae's mind, it might as well have been the skin of the last person who had trespassed in his house.

"That dress is the exact color of a trout lily blossom," Mr. Speed said. His voice was gravelly but gentle, and for some reason Lucinda Mae wanted to trust it. Lucinda Mae looked down. She was wearing her yellow corduroy dress with yellow leggings beneath. It was a long dress, to her calves. "And you," he continued. Lucinda Mae watched as the man looked at Jean now. He didn't look mad at all. Just looked surprised, maybe even pleasantly so. "You have the hair of a raven. Noble."

Before they knew what to say, he went on. "But it's wrong of you to be in my house without my permission. To what do I owe this breach of trust?"

The sound of the birds in the elm dripped into the room through the chimney or through the ceiling or walls, it was hard for Lucinda Mae to tell. She was studying the lines on Mr. Speed's cheeks. His whole face felt to her like looking at a map. "Sir," Lucinda Mae spoke finally. "A breach of trust is owed by us. We're sorry. We'd heard you lived in very strange ways in this house, and we had to see for ourselves—"

"No," he cut her off. "You don't owe a breach of trust. You apologize for a breach of trust. You're the postmaster's oldest, and you, you're the youngest of the Underwoods." Softly, he tapped his cane a few times. "So you know about right and wrong, you know about apology."

"I'm sorry," Jean said first.

"Yes, sir," Lucinda Mae added. "We're sorry."

Mr. Speed smiled at them. Lucinda Mae felt herself smiling back at the man. She wondered how similar in age he was to her Mimi.

"I hope you've accomplished your purpose. You can see that I live simply." Mr. Speed paused then, staring at the fireplace. "Would one of you please fetch some firewood from the back landing?"

Jean moved first. Lucinda Mae wondered if she should help her friend with the wood. The situation, and the man, felt oddly like a reunion, a homecoming, and she wanted to ask Jean about this, to get her opinion on it.

"You'll see the firewood out there to your right," Speed said to her. "As for you," he went on, looking at Lucinda Mae now. "I left a bag on the front porch, and as you seem to know where that is, I'd appreciate you grabbing it for me."

Thirty minutes later, the sun coming in the one west window—it wasn't a bright house—the three sat at the kitchen table, a strong little fire crackling from the hearth. "And that's the story on you two, I gather," Mr. Speed said. "Laurel Fork students, students of Miss Cartmill."

"Yes sir," Lucinda Mae said. Jean nodded in agreement. Behind her bangs, the girl looked more comfortable now. Lucinda Mae felt relief to see this. She caught her friend's eye for a moment, and in that glance she could tell that Jean wasn't disappointed at all in how their day had turned. That she was even enjoying her role of wood gatherer. Already she'd learned, as had Lucinda Mae, how to tell the difference between locust, hickory, and poplar, the poplar being good for a fast, hot burn, the locust and hickory better for, as Mr. Speed put it, "the long haul."

"I gather you all find Miss Cartmill a bit strange," Speed said. "The rest of Laurel Fork sure does."

"She's a city lady," Lucinda Mae said quickly.

"She's always calling Cinda saucy," Jean added.

"I think we make her nervous," Lucinda Mae said. A rooster crowed in the distance. There was barking, the baying of hounds. It was bear season. The hunters were running their dogs.

"Miss Cartmill is cityfolk," Mr. Speed said. "And she makes a lot of folks in Laurel Fork nervous with her ideas, her ways of teaching, the fact that she isn't married. But there are Cartmill people in these hills, and she comes from them, her grandfather does. After the war, he moved to Columbia to attend the university. And then he found work, good, paying work at a bank in Greenville after he finished at the university there." He paused and sipped from a mug of black coffee. Lucinda Mae nearly giggled aloud when she saw Jean eyeing it. And then he continued, "Matter of fact, I was out this morning doing some work for Miss Cartmill. You might think she's here like some of the other teachers you've had, the ones who sign up to work in remote places, places that some call depressed, disadvantaged. And she is, but she's here to teach for other reasons, too. She's got ambitions, good ones."

The room was warm with the fire and the light off the melting snow, and the girls were sleepy with that warmth and the excitement of their day, but when Speed suggested Miss Cartmill might be here for other reasons, their ears perked right up.

"Miss Cartmill, you've probably noticed, is very thin," he continued. "It's on account of a condition nobody can name or heal. I have some experience with helping heal folks who are ill. I do it the way my grandmother did it, with things from the woods. She was raised in some of the old ways down near Toccoa. Anyway, I was out this morning with Miss Cartmill, searching for some new items for another remedy. I've tried a number of mixes. Did you see my things in the front room?"

"I saw them," Lucinda Mae said. She noticed how there wasn't an ounce of guilt in the way she said it.

She sensed that she was right where she needed to be, right now, in order to help Miss Cartmill.

"What did you see?"

"I saw the bones and shells, stones and books and powders and things."

"These jars here, they're important, too," Mr. Speed said. "Full of roots and leaves and barks. Most thing's got medicine if you know how to get it."

"My mother makes a chamomile tea," Jean said.

"My mother likes nettle tea and dandelion tea," Lucinda Mae added.

"Those can be good for you," said Mr. Speed.

"What's the matter with Miss Cartmill?" Jean asked.

"She's sick?" Lucinda Mae added.

"She's wasting away," Mr. Speed said. "There are things going on, lots of ailments, but she's a tough lady. She tries not to let it show."

"What's saucy mean, Mr. Speed?" Jean asked.

Lucinda Mae turned and noticed that her friend's normally pale cheeks were flushed from the heat and excitement.

Mr. Speed thought a while before he spoke. Lucinda Mae watched him as he stared at the fire and then at the palms of his leathery hands. "It has, I guess, has to do with having style, a certain get up, you might say. For instance, a blue jay is more saucy than a wren. Though some would disagree."

"Does it mean the same as obnoxious?" Jean asked.

"No," Speed said. "It's more graceful than obnoxious. You can't be born obnoxious, but you can be born saucy. Most people in these parts have some sauce. It's in the water here, part of getting by."

"Lucinda Mae is always being called saucy by Miss Cartmill," Jean said.

"I can see that," Mr. Speed said. He was sitting on a wooden stool, looking at the fire. His brown eyes sparkled with the flames and with something else, too. Speed continued, spoke now as he had spoken all along, as if he was following the words with his voice. "You got any sauce, Jean?"

"She sure does," Lucinda Mae jumped in. "She's plenty saucy."

"This morning, Miss Cartmill told me you know about the Christmas that one-eyed lady got waylaid up on Painter Mountain—that so?"

What? Lucinda Mae couldn't believe her ears. Did he say, Miss Cartmill told him?

"Are you okay?" Mr. Speed asked her. Lucinda Mae felt like she'd forgotten how to speak. She glanced at Jean, who was staring at Mr. Speed like he was a ghost, and she had that 'o my gosh' face like she got when she ate too much.

"That's so," Jean said after taking a deep breath, and then turned towards her friend. "Lucinda Mae told the story, told it real good in show and tell yesterday. But nobody believed it much."

"I'm glad your Mimi told you that story, Lucinda Mae. Your Mimi is a good woman. I miss seeing her. We used to run around together in our younger years. Neither of us does much running around anymore. But you know that."

It felt like spitting up a stone she'd swallowed, but Lucinda Mae asked, "Is that story true?"

"That story is real, first off," he began. "But even with the photograph, it's hard for people to believe. Do you girls believe it?"

"I do," Lucinda Mae said quietly. She had doubted it, yes, but she was starting to see that a little doubt was part of believing. And anyway, what her Mimi said was true, she believed was true. It was normal now among her classmates to claim Santa Claus didn't exist, but Lucinda Mae had never fully let go of the chance. She doubted the other kids had either. Maybe some of them. She looked at Jean.

"It seems farfetched," Jean said. "I told my parents about it last night," she continued. "And they said it was a pretty weird story."

"Here's the way I've come to see it," Mr. Speed started. "And I've been around a while. I was there. The lady with the carriage and red dress, whether you call her Santa or what, was real. The reindeer were real, the red fox, brook trout, wild turkey, osprey, whitetail deer, and painter were real. It was all so real it was hard to believe. And now, so many years later, I don't question it. In fact, the events of that day impress me even more. That one-eyed lady, she was making do with what nature provided. Her reindeer were overheated and worn out, so she got resourceful. She found stock more suited for the weather. I call it good instincts. The world, especially now, needs more folks like that, and more stories like that, stories so true and tied to the land they're hard to believe, so hard to believe that people call them magic, call them scary, like they call these hills."

He paused for a moment. "The thing is this. In order to fix up Miss Cartmill, I've got to brew another tea. It's a strong one. I've only used it once, and that was the year your Uncle Roy, Mimi, and me helped out the one-eyed Santa. I've been without the key ingredient since then."

"What's that ingredient?" Jean asked. She was holding her head up by her palms, her elbows on the kitchen table.

"Reindeer antler," Speed said. "People way up north have brewed teas and boiled stocks of reindeer antler for hundreds of years." He looked out the west window at the flank of Painter Mountain, and he breathed a while, slow and easy. "And I believe there's a shed up there yet."

"A shed like you mean the deer shed their antlers?" Lucinda Mae wondered. She felt energized with wonder. It was like she was listening to the rules of the most excellent homework assignment in the world.

"Yes," Speed said. "But I can't get around up there on that mountain. This here leg of mine just won't do up there. It's rough country up there."

"We like rough country," Lucinda Mae jumped in. She could already see them up on the mountain, just Jean and her, looking for medicine, like old time people in the olden days. Jean shot her a glance that said hold your horses. Lucinda Mae caught her friend's glance, and smiling, said, "We sure like rough country, Mr. Speed, rough as can be."

"I suspect you do," Mr. Speed said in an amused way.

"My parents are always trying to get me to go squirrel hunting," Lucinda Mae answered. She felt strangely official, as well as eager. "They love squirrel pot pie, but they don't have time to hunt now—they're too busy with work and my baby brother."

"Nothing better than squirrel pot pie," Speed said. He stood now and took his cane and began walking around the room, circling the girls. His face changed, hardened a little. "It's no small thing to go up that mountain," he said. "Especially at this time of year. You girls are young. It is a place with a very rough beauty, very rough."

The girls stayed at the table. They looked at one another and then at the fire as they waited for Speed to continue. He had stopped moving. He stood behind them. Except for the fire, the house was quiet now. The girls heard each other breathing and the fire's hisses and snaps, and then Mr. Speed cleared his throat.

"It's a good thing we ate all that bologna," Lucinda Mae burst out.

"Sure," Jean answered.

"Bologna is good food," Speed said. "But, please, if you ever do go up that mountain, now or in the future," Mr. Speed said, his eyes calm and firm, "it's best to go together, not alone, not just one of you. He stood and started walking again. His hobble step and the thump of his cane made a kind of song. "It's time for me to rest," Speed said. "It's been good talking with you."

Lucinda Mae looked at Jean. That same rooster crowed somewhere not far up the hollow. It must have been an old rooster the way its voice crackled and waned. Jean caught Lucinda Mae's eyes, and between them passed an understanding that this Christmas was going to be some kind of adventure. In many ways, it already was.

4

Sunday came, moist and misty with mild winter air. Lucinda Mae woke early but stayed in bed listening to the birds. Her thoughts felt strong, clear, as if they'd been sifted in her sleep. She knew that Jean and she had to go up Painter Mountain. They would do it, too, she decided right then and there. Miss Cartmill deserved it. They had to do it. Lucinda Mae had been studying the water in Painter Creek for as long as she could remember, and it felt now like it had always been calling to her, the creek, its water, saying *come up the mountain, see the rough, beautiful places where I am born.*

She sat up in her bed and then reached into the side table's drawer and removed the photo her Mimi'd lent her for school. Lucinda Mae felt affection for its grainy and faded, black-and-white essence. It was beautiful, she thought, as an object, like looking at ice on a creek's edge is beautiful because it's changing and temporary. And if the one-eyed lady and the wild team of animals harnessed to her carriage were not quite in focus, they felt more real to the girl as a result. The reindeer were like blobs, hard to see, but she could tell where the antlers stood, and she could see the corral's posts clearly, too, spaced about ten feet apart. The sun was coming from behind the camera. There were no ridgelines in the distance, only gray sky; this was certainly the top of Painter Mountain. The mountain had burned back then, and there were charred stumps, chunks of tree. Lucinda Mae felt a lonesomeness as she focused on evidence of the fire's changes to the land. She remembered the photo had been taken in 1946. It was thirty-three years old. There was, she noticed, a rock slab on the ground not far from the corral, and it was large, extended beyond the photo's border. Lucinda Mae figured the soil had worn off of there, if there ever had been soil. Lucinda Mae studied the image for other landmarks, but nothing stood out with the same power.

Lucinda Mae's mind chugged along, earnest and intent as running water. She knew that even if Jean and she didn't find the reindeer antler, they would be helping Miss Cartmill simply by trying. She wanted that, to try to help. Miss Cartmill had always fascinated and frightened her. But now the teacher held a more intimate role. She was a person who needed Lucinda Mae's help. It was strange. She felt glad to know more about Mr. Speed, as well. Lucinda Mae had never expected his privacy to contain good things besides the opportunities to make up funny stories about him.

Lucinda Mae was moving now, and after she made the bed and dressed, she brushed her hair. She didn't care for mirrors or have one in her room, so she brushed her hair at the window each morning. She wondered who built the window, and where, and simultaneously she rode another train of thought that carried the idea that the mist was Painter Mountain's breath. She smiled. She felt especially good today. Her hair was tangled, as usual, and pulled on her scalp as she brushed it. She was still learning ways to make this morning ritual less painful.

Soon enough, she heard her baby brother crying and thought of what she might fix for breakfast after feeding her chickens. She decided on frog in a hole, a piece of bread with a hole torn in it, an egg fried in the middle of that hole. This was her Mimi's favorite breakfast. Her Mimi had showed her the simple but yummy meal some years back. She thought of her Mimi, those attentive and sometimes feisty ways she had. Lucinda Mae played with the idea of telling her about Mr. Speed and Miss Cartmill and the reindeer antler. Her Mimi might give Jean and her some needed advice. There were two days until Christmas Eve, and Lucinda Mae knew that another snowfall would make finding the reindeer antler nearly impossible, but the mild winter air suggested little chance of snow. No matter what, she knew they had to go up the mountain and search for the antler as soon as they could. She decided to check in with Jean at church, do some planning and also do, to use a Miss Cartmill word, some brainstorming. She hoped she could catch up with her for a private few moments either before or after the service.

Lucinda Mae was pleased to find two eggs in the henhouse when she entered to fill the old gutter that served as a feed trough. Along with the dozen eggs she'd been gathering in the evenings, a couple in the morning made a fair fetch for this time of year. She noticed some annoyance in the pitch of her hens' clucks and cackles. The wet snow limited their movement. Their bedding was damp with mist. Everything was soaked. Melt dripped from the shed roof. A few stubborn hens pecked at the mud in the chicken yard and then stood tall, as if hoping to see grass and bugs instead of mucky slush.

For a while, Lucinda Mae sat under the eave and looked at her favorite old oak just up the hill, its damp bark, its limbs and buds framed against the mist. She heard her father giving food and water to the hogs that would be meat in the freezer before the new year. A bundle of dead leaves hung from a high branch's fork. Lichen, a soft lime color, splotched the bark, growing thickest at the limbs' outer reaches, and it reminded her of the time Jean got into her cousin Sarah's makeup kit and painted the faces of her dolls. That was a few years ago, and it still made her smile to think of it. Now the variety of shades in the remaining snow turned her mind to reindeer antler. How strange here in the Gorges to be thinking of reindeer at all. But so be it. Her father and his friends kept the racks of whitetail bucks they took during hunting season. They hadn't used the antlers for food. She wondered what nourishment they contained. That the woods were full of mysteries was nothing new to Lucinda Mae. It was as if the creek had been whispering them to her for many years, but only now might she be ready to hear them.

A couple of hours later, the snowpack had shrunk to small patches. It was forty-five degrees, the sunlight harsh and inviting both, low in the sky as it was. Lucinda Mae thought it was strange that she hadn't seen Jean and her family in church. She wondered if they'd arrived late, sat in the back, and then left early. Now she was on her way out of church, following her parents, Peanut in her mom's arms, when Jean's cousin Joy Underwood stopped her to relate the the news. Jean's Uncle Larry had taken a bad fall off a ladder on a job and was in the hospital down in Greenville. That morning, Jean and the rest of her family had driven over to be with him. They were going to spend a couple of days there, helping the family and looking after her Uncle. They wouldn't return until late Christmas Eve.

"Christmas Eve," Lucinda Mae muttered. She was stunned.

Joy saw Lucinda Mae turn thoughtful. "Do you know her uncle?" she asked.

"No," said Lucinda Mae. "I mean, I met him a couple of times. It's a real shame he's hurt. How bad is it?"

"It's his back," Joy said. "It's bad but not too bad. He was lucky." Lucinda Mae was only partly listening as Joy kept talking. She'd noticed Miss Cartmill across the way, in her brown pantsuit. Her teacher was walking with her head down and with a limp. She looked serious, too hurried and out of sorts for a bright winter Sunday after church. Lucinda Mae felt a great stirring as she looked at her teacher. She wanted to run over and tell her that she and Jean were going to try to help her.

"That's bad but good, I guess," Lucinda Mae said once Joy finished talking. She felt the sudden urge now to run and give Miss Cartmill a big hug. "Tell everyone we're thinking of them, would you?"

"Yes, I will," Joy said.

"Thank you," Lucinda Mae said. Her parents were headed to the church lunch, opposite the direction of Miss Cartmill. It was time to catch up with them.

⊰ ⊱

Lucinda Mae liked Sunday afternoons. They were slow, quiet days around the Coggins home. They reminded her of Mrs. Norwood's oyster stew from the church lunch, warm and hearty and nourishing; she'd eaten two big bowls of it today. Her father rested on the couch. Lucinda Mae's mother, also in the family room, worked on a letter at the desk while the baby slept on his dad's chest. Lucinda Mae, meanwhile, felt less relaxed. She sat at her desk in her room, studying Mr. Speed's map of Painter Mountain. She didn't like it but there was no option; she would have to go up the mountain without Jean. Lucinda Mae worked to focus her thoughts in a positive way about her adventure. Painter Mountain was, in effect, she told herself, just her backyard, or an extension of it. She thought of how she knew the mountain day in and day out, through talk of family and friends and through her own poking around the lower flanks of it. She'd also seen one tiny patch of it in her Mimi's photograph. And how she knew it through the creek, which carried its silt and sand and whispered its mysteries to her each school morning as she waited for the bus.

She looked now out her bedroom window at Painter Mountain, and thought of how it changed with the seasons. How the old roadbeds from the logging days were sometimes visible after a snowfall. How, in summer, the mountain was a green mass. In spring and fall it resembled the banana bread her Aunt Janet made. She loved to study the mountain in all seasons, but she especially liked to watch the leaves bud out on the trees at the mountain's lower slopes first and then move upwards in spring. In the fall, the trees lost their leaves from the top downwards. It was always a good bit cooler, she knew, in the mountain's upper reaches where the corral was, the weather more severe.

She looked back now at Mr. Speed's map. It was detailed. There were important landmarks. He had noted the old mine tailings, the logging roads, and certain drainages, flats, and hollows. The corral looked to be a few miles up. It wasn't going to be hard to find the corral, but to find the reindeer antler under all the leaf duff and fallen trees, to do that was going to require more than luck. She wished Jean was with her now, so they could talk about it together. She wished she had Jean's eyes.

Lucinda Mae decided to check to see if Mimi might share some details about the mountain and the reindeer. She knew she'd gotten all the help Mr. Speed could give her, through the conversation in the kitchen but mostly from the map itself, and decided that she needed to ask her Mimi about the old photo. She would do so in a roundabout way, so her Mimi wouldn't know that she was thinking of going up there.

Her Mimi lived in a trailer across the driveway with a Fyce hound named Hoss. Hoss was eleven but still pretty spry. Mimi was not a churchgoer. Lucinda Mae often visited with her on Sunday afternoons, when she was likely to be in the mood for chatting a while, and maybe a few games of checkers. Lucinda Mae decided now that an offering to Mimi of something good to eat might help her luck with all of this reindeer business. She'd noticed a bundle of old bananas in the fruit bowl this morning. Mimi liked banana bread almost as much as Lucinda Mae felt like baking now, and she also knew how mixing a batter always helped settle the many things in her heart.

❧ ❧

Lucinda Mae had just finished blending the lard, maple syrup, and grated lemon rind into a creamy mix when her father appeared in the kitchen.

"What are you up to, Miss Mae?" he asked. He wore a warm, rested smile, which scrunched his blue eyes behind the thick glasses that nearly always covered them.

"Banana bread," Lucinda Mae said as she beat the eggs and mashed banana into the mix. "That's good," her father said. He was at the sink, starting to wash the dishes she no longer needed. He hummed a slow tune.

"I hope it turns out okay," Lucinda Mae muttered

after a while. She had filled three greased bread pans and was about to load them in the oven. She wondered if she was talking more about the bread or her journey up the mountain, but told herself to stop it, that Painter Mountain was her backyard, and it was no big deal for a girl to explore her backyard.

"Never had a thing of yours that wasn't okay," her dad said. Lucinda Mae felt warm inside on hearing this praise, but she snickered all the same. There were plenty of burnt cookies in her recent past. And more than once had she mistaken baking soda for baking powder, giving her goodies a metallic bite. Her father was generous with praise, and it bothered her sometimes, the distance it kept between them.

"Dad," Lucinda Mae said, looking at him in his comfy old jeans and a soft, faded-blue postal service shirt that had been washed too many times to be fit for wearing to work

"Yes," her dad said.

"Can I take the .20 gauge for a squirrel hunt tomorrow?" the girl asked. In the pause that followed, Lucinda Mae saw many stories in her dad's face. She knew how much he valued that gun, the family heirloom. He scrubbed the mixing bowl like there was something buried in it.

"Where you want to hunt?" he asked.

"Just up in the woods, up on Painter," Lucinda Mae said.

"Ought to be a good day for it," he said. "I hope you have some luck." Lucinda Mae was relieved, though she knew he liked for his daughter to hunt squirrel. She knew, also, that he trusted her to be safe in the woods and with the gun. They had started hunting together when she was six. For the first two years, she hadn't carried a gun but sat with him or walked and watched. He trained her up, showing her the ways of the woods. He taught her how to walk in them after game, be safe with the gun, and how to clean it, all its parts, very well. When he took her shooting, first with a .22 for a paper target drawn on an old cardboard box, she had been a quick study, as he called it. The next time she shot, it was in the woods at a big gray squirrel, and she'd missed, a clean miss. The next time after that, she killed a gray fluff tail with a tough shot high in the crotch of the oak out by the chicken yard. She'd watched her father clean the animal and then helped clean the three he'd taken. She killed four more squirrels the next winter, the last two while hunting on her own the week after Christmas. It wasn't the killing that she liked about hunting, it was the quiet attention. Her favorite hunts were often the ones where she came back with no squirrel except for those she'd imagined seeing.

↢ ↣

"You're the mother of all mothers, girl!" Mimi said when she opened the door to the smiling, slightly sheepish face of Lucinda Mae. The smell of hot banana bread filled the air. Hoss barked and nipped at Lucinda Mae's rubber boots. When Mimi closed her eyes and breathed in the thick, sweet smell, Lucinda Mae saw that her Mimi was wearing a denim dress over a white turtleneck. On her feet were her beloved house slippers.

"Hi, Mimi."

"Don't you hi me. Get your yellow dress wearing, red headed sweetness in here where it's warm."

"It's warm out here, Mimi."

"Just get in here, girl."

Lucinda Mae obeyed. Hoss ran off across the yard, yapping like there was no tomorrow, no yesterday either. The girl sensed that her Mimi was in one of her wild moods. This visit could be interesting, she thought. "And let me get a knife and some plates. That there in your paws smells like the breath of the only angels I ever want to know."

Lucinda Mae entered the long, narrow home. It was musty with oil heat turned way too high. Someone on the television blabbered in the background. There was the same stack of newspapers by the sofa, only the pile was larger than the girl remembered. "Come on in here," her Mimi said. "Let's get checkers and see who's still got a brain."

"Mimi," Lucinda Mae said. "I can't stay long. Mama needs me to watch Peanut soon." Mimi smiled. "Then you fetch him over here, too. We'll teach him checkers. It'll do him some good."

"He's ten months old, Mimi."

"That's plenty old for checkers," her Mimi said. "I remember playing checkers in my ma's belly."

"You're something saucy," Lucinda Mae said to her Mimi just as the woman placed a thick slice of banana bread on a plate for her. The girl looked at her grandmother. Beneath her short, graying hair, the woman's face had turned curious.

"Did you call me saucy?"

Lucinda Mae hesitated. She had a feeling she might have insulted her Mimi. "Yes, I did."

"That's a marvel. See, that's just the word I was looking for in my Sunday crossword." Her Mimi paused, stared out the window as she chewed the warm bread. "A boy I knew years ago, Frankie Cartmill, he used that word like you use those yellow dresses, day in and day out." Somebody was laughing on the television now. It was a scary laugh, like the person was more fearful than amused. Lucinda Mae took another bite of her bread and decided, yet again, that life was weird, and good.

"Do you have a dictionary?" Lucinda Mae asked her Mimi.

"Does a hobby horse have a hickory eyeball? A crossword lady without a dictionary is like, I don't know, but it's right there by the newspapers. A dictionary is my pantry when it comes to crosswording." Lucinda Mae, in two lunge steps, fetched the grey, tattered book. "You looking up saucy?" her Mimi asked.

"Yes, ma'am."

"It means saucy. Saucy means saucy, no more and no less. Any other definition is just words. You know saucy when you see it. Saucy pours all over you. Like any sauce, it can be good or it can be bad." Lucinda Mae was half listening as she flipped the thin pages of the dictionary. A strange word at the top of the page caught her eye: "satyr," some sort of goat-human thingamajig. But just down the page was the word she wanted.

Lucinda Mae read the definition out loud, "Impertinently bold and impudent, amusingly forward and flippant."

"Sounds like the word means," said her Mimi.

"Sounds rude," Lucinda Mae said.

"I didn't hear that word in the definition," Mimi said with a mouthful of banana bread. She swallowed and continued, pointing her delicate, waxy finger, "Where's the word come from?" Lucinda Mae looked up.

"It comes from my teacher. She says it a lot."

"No," Mimi said, reaching for the dictionary. Lucinda Mae handed it to her. The thick book was still open to page 1044 with its headings, "*sassafras * satyagraha*," and page 1045's "*satyr * savvy*." "Here's what I mean," her Mimi said. "Up here under sauce, the etymology, the roots of the word, its origins. It comes from the Latin for 'salt.'"

"Salt?"

"That's right, girl," her Mimi said, biting into her bread. "Salt." There was a pause. Water dripped with a clock's precision out the window, each drop catching the low winter light—sparkle, sparkle, sparkle. The window, Lucinda Mae noticed, needed washing. "Like 'skillet licker' comes from 'skill.' Your granddaddy was such an eater that even from tike's age everybody called him the skillet licker."

"I'll set up the checkers," the girl said. She was smiling at the skillet licker stuff. "Sound okay, Mimi?"

"Okay."

Lucinda Mae took the red pieces and Mimi the black. As the first game moved swiftly to a draw, Lucinda Mae gathered herself for asking Mimi about the photo and Painter Mountain. She knew Mimi would have wisdom, and she trusted that Mimi would gift her with it.

"Show and tell went well on Friday," she said. "I took that picture of the one-eyed lady and all the animals and told the story you told me."

"You can't go wrong with that story."

"No, ma'am. But it's strange that it could be true."

"That was some warm winter," Mimi muttered. "That's the truth." The old woman stared at the game, planned a move. "Girl, I know it's hard to believe. Even with a photograph. I understand it's hard to believe." Mimi paused a moment. She was deep in thought. "Let me tell you something," she started, and looked up from the checkers game right hard into Lucinda Mae's eyes. "This is something I've never told a soul. That lady, I'll call her Red Dress, I swear on my grand-mama's Bible, had only one eye, that is all, one eye."

"That's in the picture, her one eye," Lucinda Mae said.

"I know it was, girl," her Mimi said, excited in a more serious way than usual, "but listen on, you gotta hear this. The one-eye was the eye on the right, look-ing at her, and it was a small, strange eye. I couldn't see her one eye as you see other people's eyes. And the place where her other eye should have been was only skin. Pale skin had grown over the place where her other eye should have been. So I asked her about it.

Mimi's voice grew hushed and dramatic as she continued, and she looked at Lucinda Mae like she'd never felt looked at before, "Red Dress said, 'It is so, I only have one eye.' She smiled, and continued, "but it is a good eye.' Red Dress laughed then. She nearly snorted with laughter. Her head bounced like a bush with an animal in it, and I saw that her one eye was set far inside the place where eyes are set, that place they call the eye socket. It looked so different from any eye I'd seen. Red Dress started again, 'I'll tell you the story of my eye. I can see that it interests you, and I can see that you are to be trusted. Years ago, many years ago, indeed, I did not live in the North Pole. I lived in a tropical island, in the crater of a dormant volcano among jungle and estuary, sea and reef. You see, I did not use a carriage in those decades. There was no snow there for a carriage. I used a boat, a really fine, sturdy boat, and a team of dolphins pulled it. It was a delightful country, and in the long stretches of time between Christmas Eves, when I wasn't busy working, I would explore the jungle and the estuaries and the seacoast. I loved that country. The places and people and critters inspired me to make the gifts I made, to keep up with my work. It was dense country, rich and full of wonders.

Lucinda Mae felt completely lost in the story, lost in her Mimi's brown eyes, too, whose stare she met without hardly blinking. She felt like she was standing right next to Mimi listening to Red Dress way back when. Now her Mimi continued, her voice rising and falling like water over rocks, and Lucinda Mae continued to meet her Mimi's gaze,

'One day, and this was a long time ago—I am older than anyone can know—I met a man. He was a good man and possessed a strange power. He could send his eyes out of his head. I do not lie. Here was this man on the jungle floor, and he would send his eyes up to the top of one of those giant tropical trees so he could see the view from there. Or he could send his eyes down under the water of the sea or the rivers and see what the fish and crabs were doing.

'I asked the man to teach me how to do this. The man taught me then, but he warned me not to do it more than three times in a day. So I went off along the trail at the base of the volcano. When I came to the first big tree I could find, I sent my eyes to the top of it. And I saw for miles. And then I called my eyes back and went along the trail. This was an amazing new ability, this power of vision, and I was entranced by it, too entranced. Later, I sent my eyes on a lizard's back, and I saw many wonderful things. Then after that, I sent my eyes on the wings of a great seabird, and I saw more than I can say. The fourth time I did this my eyes remained fastened to the limb of the tallest tree in all the jungle. I called my eyes back. They did not come. All day and through the night, I called. They did not return to me, my eyes. I grew tired and sad, and I wept. Really, I was less sad than angry with myself for being greedy. I had not used my gift as I had been told to use it. Also, I was scared. I had no eyes! Heavy with sadness and anger and many other emotions, I laid down and slept, crying even in my sleep. Tears poured from where my eyes had been. I was half asleep and still weeping when a little monkey ran over my face. There are lots of monkeys in the jungle forest. I closed my lids so the monkey would not see that I was blind, and I lay still so as to catch him. At last, the monkey sat upon my chest. I stayed quiet. The monkey grew used to me and started to pluck strands of my hair, perhaps for its nest or just to play with. Monkeys are curious animals. Soon this monkey began to lick my tears; they were not completely dry. Its tail hung near my mouth, which I closed, snapped shut, catching the monkey. I held the tail tightly in my teeth.' Lucinda Mae felt her face stretch as her eyes grew big at this detail. Mimi spoke like she had something in her mouth, and kept looking deep in Lucinda Mae's eyes. 'The monkey tried to escape but could not. After a little while, the monkey listened as I told it to guide me to my eyes. The monkey said it could see my eyes in the tallest tree. It said that my eyes had swelled to an enormous size. The size of a crocodile bladder, it said. The monkey offered to climb the tree and get them for me, but I would not let it go. Monkeys are tricky animals. It tried to pull free then, it tried hard, but I held its tail hard between my teeth. Then the monkey asked on what condition would I set it free. I said only if it would give me one of its eyes. So it gave me one of its eyes, and I could see again, blurrily, as though I was looking through stained glass or flames, and I let the monkey go.'

"Red Dress stopped talking then, and I was relieved to see her look back to her carriage, the reindeer, and Painter Mountain. As she'd told the story she'd looked intently at me, and as I'd listened I had faithfully returned her strange, one-eyed gaze. "That is an amazing story," I said to Red Dress. "If I was not looking at you, at your face, I would not believe it."

'It is a true story,' Red Dress said. 'The truth is strange.'

"I looked at Red Dress then. I sensed that she had more to say. Suddenly, she looked hard at me. She opened her one eye as big as it could open, which wasn't very big. 'You need to know that I have not told that story before, and that you can tell that story to one person, one and only one, but do not tell it to another, and tell that one person to do the same, not to tell it to more than one person. Do you understand?'

"'I understand,' I said to Red Dress. And I did understand, and I haven't told anyone until now, Lucinda Mae. You must not repeat this story, Lucinda Mae, to more than one person."

"I hear you," Lucinda Mae said, but she knew she was doing more than hearing her; she was completely in another time and place with her, that time and place, feeling her and Red Dress, everything, like she was there.

"Good," said her Mimi. "Now, and you probably are wondering this yourself, I had a question for Red Dress. 'Why do you live in the North Pole now?' I asked her. Why did you leave the tropical island?"

'That is a good question,' Red Dress said. 'I will tell you two of the many reasons.'

'With only one eye, and a monkey eye at that, I could not see so well. I have learned to see better since those early days, but the jungle is a crowded place. I could not move around without bumping into things. There are things in a jungle you don't want to bump, things with stingers and poison and sharp teeth.

'Also, and maybe more importantly, the place where my other eye had been was now like an open wound. There are many germs in warm places, and the wound would not heal. So the good dolphins pulled me part of the way to the North Pole. Then the whales did the pulling. It was hard to leave my homeplace. I had lived there my whole life, as had generations of my family before me. It was necessary, though. So I said goodbye to everyone and everything I knew. The dolphins and whales pulled my boat with all my belongings up and through the increasingly cold waters to my present home among the ice, where there is little to bump into, few trees, few rocks, and so forth. Up there, the wound of my former eye has healed just fine.'"

Lucinda Mae smiled at her grandmother's words. There were strange feels in her chest and in her forehead, too. "Mimi?"

"Yes."

"That's some story. Thank you for telling me that."

"Keep that story safe, girl," Mimi said. "The truth has lots of nooks and crannies, doesn't it?"

"It does, Mimi," the girl said, "and I'll keep it safe, yes, ma'am." There was a long moment of quiet before Lucinda Mae asked, "How well do you know Mr. Speed?"

"I knew him well. That was back a few years," Mimi said as she jumped one of Lucinda Mae's red checkers. All through the story of Red Dress, Mimi had not made her checker move. Now the game was back in swing.

As they played, Lucinda Mae tried to ask her Mimi everything she could ask about Speed and Red Dress without giving away her plan to go up the mountain. She sensed that her Mimi wouldn't be opposed to it, but she didn't want to risk it. In fact, the longer she sat with the plan, and the more questions she asked her Mimi, the more she felt convinced that it had to be just her's. There was something about the independence of it that felt important to Lucinda Mae. They played another whole game. Mimi nodded her head as she listened and responded to Lucinda Mae's questions, and her face grew serious. She played her checkers with less skill than usual. The girl sensed that the talk was taking up some space in her head.

"Do you think there's a reindeer antler up there?" Lucinda Mae asked.

Mimi didn't say anything right off. She set up her black checkers for another game. The sound of the wood discs on the cardboard wasn't much different from the sound of the drip out the window.

"Miss Lucinda," her Mimi finally said. The old lady was still. She stared at her granddaughter hard in the eye. And then she started clearing the checkerboard. "Listen," she said. "I want you run out to the shed and fetch me one of your pop's deer antlers."

"Right now?" the girl asked.

"Right away," said her Mimi. "And bring little Hoss back in here with you, too."

When Lucinda Mae returned with the antler and the dog, Mimi was on the sofa. The television was off. "Bring me that, darling."

Lucinda Mae did as she was told. Hoss followed. He acted curious about the antler. Lucinda Mae smiled at him, his little white body, those funny patches of brown hair around his eyes. "Hoss, you old rascal," her Mimi said. "Take a good chew on this."

The dog took the antler in his mouth. The jagged weight was too much for him to carry, but he dragged it under the kitchen table, where he let it go and sniffed it up and down.

"That's what I expected," Mimi said.

"What?" Lucinda Mae asked.

"You know this little Hoss has quite a nose," Mimi said. "If there were reindeer antler up there, think of all the animals that would have found them by now. Hoss would have found them, too, if the coyotes and squirrels and bobcat and stuff hadn't. Hoss used to run up there a lot, back a while ago."

Lucinda Mae nodded but she felt a little like crying. She watched little Hoss. He was licking the antler at its butt end, the warty and flared part. She felt a wave of helplessness flow through her, and then a lot of waves.

Then Mimi looked out the window. Lucinda Mae followed her grandmother's eyes. Long shadows of the trees against the remaining snow made the hillside look like a wicker mound. The drip was slower than earlier. They had a good, slow look out the window together before her Mimi said, "You come by here and fetch him before you go squirrel hunting."

"I'll do that, Mimi," Lucinda Mae said. "Thank you."

"And thank you for the banana bread and the visit," her Mimi responded. "You get home now. It's getting on Sunday suppertime."

"Yes, ma'am," Lucinda Mae said. On her way to the door, she knelt down to give Hoss a pet on the head but the dog growled, possessive about the antler.

Lucinda Mae could still hear her Mimi giggling at Hoss's growling as she shut the door.

⊹ ⊹

On the way home, Lucinda Mae stopped to give her hens their evening feed. She thought of Jean as she did her job. She hoped that Jean's Uncle Larry was okay. Lucinda Mae admitted to herself that she was more than a little nervous about her day tomorrow, knowing she would be alone. She needed Jean. The mountain was the tallest in the state, known for its strange rock formations, cliffs and caves, and known also for being home to many wild things. She'd seen the deer, turkeys, foxes, opossum, bobcat, coyote, and bear while hunting and even in her yard and in the road. Often she saw these critters in the headlights, driving with her parents. A few months back, a 500 pound black bear had tore up Mr. Underwood's bee hives. The next night he tried to break into Lucinda Mae's chicken house to get at the feed. Her dad had to spend several hours on repairs. It was good of Mimi to be sending Hoss with her, but he wasn't the same as Jean.

Lucinda Mae came into the kitchen, holding the hem of her yellow dress, thirteen eggs in the fold of that thick cotton. Her mama was at the counter, mixing a bowl of meat. Pink and burgundy, it looked like a mix of pork sausage and ground venison. "Meat loaf tonight," her mama said.

"Yum," Lucinda Mae said as she placed the eggs, one at a time, in a wire storage basket.

"How's Mimi?" her ma asked.

"She's feisty today."

"Nice feisty?"

"Yes, nice feisty."

"Cinda, would you check on Peanut? He's in the living room. Your dad ran up to the Underwood's to see to the bees and feed the dog. They had to go out of town."

"I heard that. I heard Jean's uncle got hurt."

"It's too bad," her mom said.

"Yes," Lucinda Mae said.

Peanut was not her baby brother's given name. His name was David, like his dad, but he'd been Peanut ever since her Mimi called him that soon after he was born. He didn't look anything like a peanut, Lucinda Mae thought as she knelt over where he lay on the carpet. His big brown eyes fixed on hers, and she smiled. He smiled back. She started giggling. He squirmed, sat up, and then laid down again. He had only recently taken to sitting up. Lucinda Mae grabbed his socked feet in her hands and made like he was running, extending each leg slow at first and then faster. Now he giggled, too, and she laughed and cooed at him and sang, "Here comes the Peanut man, the Peanut man, the Peanut man. Here comes the Peanut man, running to kiss me." And then she plopped a big smooch on his cheek.

He laughed and squirmed. Lucinda Mae played with him like this until it was time for meatloaf.

A while after dinner, Lucinda Mae still felt good and full from the meatloaf, full as the moon that shone through a long and thin salamander-shaped cloud. The girl lay in bed in her yellow nightgown. She listened to the slow drip of the last melt off the roof, and she stared at the moon out her window. Before bed, she'd found in her encyclopedia photos of reindeer with antlers. She'd studied the antlers' shapes for a while, and then she'd drawn them several times in her diary. She wanted her eyes trained should she see an antler in the woods.

Meanwhile, she wondered about something her father had said while doing the dishes. In the post office on Friday, Mr. Walker had mentioned spotting a painter, a panther, up the road one night the prior week. Her father had assured Lucinda Mae and her mother that it was likely a bobcat or a coyote, that Mr. Walker was an older gentleman and his eyesight wasn't great. But it was hard for Lucinda Mae not to wonder. Eventually, she fell asleep. She slept hard. Her dreams were various and colorful, but in the morning she wouldn't remember them. She would be getting up early, before dawn, to pack herself lunch and snacks for a day on the mountain. She wanted to get an early start.

5

The wind picked up overnight. It howled out of the northwest, whistling and purring against the house siding and window frames. The sky was clear, the air colder. Nothing dripped. Lucinda Mae woke before her alarm. It was five 'o seven. She fought the urge to stay in bed and instead dressed in long johns and her thickest yellow wool dress, and then pulled herself into her yellow turtleneck sweater, too. As she dressed she thought of the reindeer antler pictures she'd studied, and of the map of the mountain, and of all the things Mr. Speed and Mimi had said. She paused after pulling on two pairs of wool socks, the thin pair against her skin, the thick pair over that, and she looked out the window toward the mountain, which was still shrouded in darkness. "Please be good to me, Painter Mountain," she said quietly.

"There's my squirrel hunter," her father said when she crept into the kitchen. She didn't want to wake Peanut or her mother.

"Good morning, Dad," Lucinda Mae said. He nodded on his way to add a few chunks of locust to the woodstove. Lucinda Mae got busy; it was the easiest way to resist the nervousness about her mission today. She packed a loaf of banana bread in foil. In more foil, she wrapped a healthy length of the venison bologna she loved so well, and some leftover meatloaf, a chunk of cheddar. She saw a tin cup while looking for crackers, and she put that in her knapsack for drinking out of springs. A lot of water ran off of Painter Mountain. The crackers she packed in the cup to keep them from crumbling.

Her father had been watching her. "Why don't you take these, too?"

Lucinda Mae looked at him. He was dressed in his postal service uniform. He appeared clean, presentable, and tired, and he was holding a single sheath of fig bars. "Yum," the girl said. "Thanks. I love these."

Her dad gave her a peck on the cheek and headed out the door for work. She didn't notice until he left that he'd placed the gun in its sock on the kitchen table, as well as the orange hunting vest, its pockets full of .20 gauge squirrel loads. He had also left a big helping of oatmeal in the pot on the stove. She ate a good share, and ate it slowly, knowing it's energy would help her on the mountain, and then she started to wash the dishes just as her mother appeared with a smile on her face. "My hunter girl," her mom said.

Lucinda Mae reached for a good morning hug. "I know you like squirrel, Mom."

"That I do."

Lucinda Mae felt grateful. Even if it made her nervous, she knew she was lucky to be able to go out on her own. It wasn't unusual among her friends and classmates that a girl hunted, but it was rare that they were able to go alone. Lucinda Mae had earned her parents' trust, but she also understood that it didn't take any special effort, that it came natural for her to be responsible because her parents had allowed her responsibility early on. They'd raised her such, letting her do the stuff of life right alongside them. They didn't baby her. She remembered how at age seven they'd let her help work up a flock of her Aunt Janet's meat birds. There were other people present, and they commented on how she dressed the plump chickens with unusual skill. But Lucinda Mae was just watching and doing what they were doing. It wasn't anything tricky.

"Thank you for letting me go out today," Lucinda Mae said to her mother.

"You're very welcome," her mother said. "You be sure and take care of your father's gun. You know how much he values it."

"I will," Lucinda Mae said. "And please give Peanut a smooch for me when he wakes."

"I'll do that."

Lucinda Mae finished wrapping her neck in a scarf, and then layered her upper body against the cold. There was room in her knapsack should she need to strip a coat or sweater.

"Bye, Mom," she said. "See you later."

Her mother nodded, busy with morning things. Lucinda Mae went into the cold dawn.

First she stole up the creek to Speed's, pausing a few times to stare up the mountain as the morning light grew in the east. She took the same creek path that Jean and she walked on Saturday when all this business came about. The sun was not yet over the ridge, and it was cold, but the girl was warm in her winter clothes, and there was plenty of light to see her way. She held the side by side .20 gauge over her shoulder. She felt strong. It was still too early for the squirrels to be moving. But soon as that sun shone, she knew they'd be about.

She thought of Jean. She missed Jean. She knew she was thinking of her as a way to bring her presence near. She thought of the way Jean and she had laughed on the bus home from school on Friday. Hal Kessler had been seated behind them, and when the bus was pulling into the school, they'd overheard Hal telling his pal Tommy Grimes how they weren't going to have a Christmas tree this year but Hal was going to dress in a forest green sweater and forest green jeans and a pointy green stocking hat, and then stand with his arms out. They were going to hang ornaments from his clothes. Hal had been joshing, but you never knew with the Kesslers. Mr. Kessler had come back to the Gorges after working as a drummer in a rock 'n roll band. He'd been all over the world with the band, playing what some called swamp rock to thousands and thousands of people. At least, that's how Hal told the story. It appeared true when you saw Mr. Kessler. He wore his hair long. He wore earrings and tight, flower-embroidered denim pants that flared at the base. Lucinda Mae thought such pants looked better on Miss Cartmill than on Mr. Kessler, but she liked Hal. He was funny and he was also nice. He didn't throw around all that rude talk that a lot of the boys at school did.

The creek had dropped overnight since the melt of the prior day and the subsequent freeze again after dark. There was ice on the rocks and logs where it had still run swollen in the early part of the night. Lucinda Mae saw all kinds of faces in the ice shapes. The morning light shifted and slithered through the oblong, jagged formations. It was lovely. Lucinda Mae's insulated rubber boots were quiet on the hard ground, except where she stepped on the old snow and they crunched. She moved with efficiency. Thinking of Jean and Hal and the Kesslers had comforted her. She felt ready for anything.

Not far from Speed's place, the girl hunkered behind the rootball of a blown down tree. To her right rose a big shagbark with a squirrel hole twenty feet up the west side. She watched and waited. She had seen squirrels up there before. It would make a clean shot, she noticed, no houses or road beyond, just more woods. She loaded both barrels of the side by side and made herself still. The sky brightened slowly. She thought of Miss Cartmill and of the old photograph and all that it contained and didn't contain. She thought of the mountain, its mysteries, and of antler, whether there might really be a shed one, and where. After a few minutes, a pileated woodpecker came bobbing through the canopy and lit on the dead branch of a nearby oak. She loved the red heads of these big birds. Lucinda Mae watched it drill at the branch. When she looked back at the hole, she noticed a squirrel seated in the crotch of the limb just up from its den's opening. She almost scolded herself for being distracted by the pileated, but caught herself, and in one fluid motion, she flicked off the safety and reached with her finger to the left barrel's trigger, meanwhile mounting the gun stock to her shoulder. She placed the bead on the squirrel and fired. The morning changed. When her ears cleared, she heard the pileated screaming as it flew away. The sun was full over the southeastern ridge now.

Lucinda Mae was grateful for a clean kill. She stashed the squirrel in the game pocket of her orange vest and then unloaded her gun. She felt the way she always felt after taking a life, that strange mix of dread and power, humility and thanks, though she wouldn't have called it that. She felt closer to the world than she'd felt in a long time, almost too close, and she said a silent prayer. How weird death was, how much a part of life. The girl remembered Baylus Albert, a quiet and athletic kid in her class who was buried in the grave-yard last winter after a bad car accident, but mostly she thought of his family and how tough it must have been, how tough it still must be. As she thought of Baylus, her mind simultaneously returned to Miss Cartmill and her illness. She felt a mix of compassion, doubt, hope, and fear about her teacher and the possibility that, of all things, Old Man Speed and a reindeer antler from Painter Mountain, as well as Jean and her, might be of help.

Lucinda Mae was planning to head up the mountain at a place some distance from Mr. Speed's yard. There was a drainage that way, one of the many tributaries of Painter Creek. As she moved that direction, she realized she'd forgotten to get Hoss from her Mimi *and* had overlooked her duty to the chickens. She stomped the ground with her right foot and shook her head. You're as forgetful as can be, she said in her mind, putting on her best Jean Underwood voice. But it was probably for the best, she decided, knowing her Mimi was not the early riser she used to be when she worked at the old button factory. Once more, Lucinda Mae followed the path through the growth along the creek, Jean and her footprints from the day before still frozen in the little remaining snow.

Lucinda Mae was telling herself to take it easy when she saw Jean standing ahead in the trail with a strange smile on her face. Lucinda Mae felt an immediate urge to run up to her and, as her Mimi sometimes said, hug the tar out of her.

"I heard you shoot!" Jean said. She was smiling. "Get one?"

Lucinda Mae nodded. "I'm happy to see you. How's your Uncle Larry?"

"He's okay," Jean said. "Not great. Just okay."

"I'm glad you're back," Lucinda Mae said, her voice tense with excitement. You know where we're going today, right?"

Lucinda Mae watched Jean's eyes shut as she looked with pursed lips down. Then, when Jean looked up, her eyes opened and she smiled with grim determination, her mouth closed, teeth clenched. Finally, Jean said, "I think I do."

"Good, but you look like you might want to run

home and fetch some better clothes," Lucinda Mae said. "And better shoes, too."

Jean's smile loosened and she reached for Lucinda Mae's hand, took it in her own and held it tightly. "You're bringing the snacks, right?"

They both smiled. Lucinda Mae knew that Jean taking her hand was a way for her friend to tell her to not fall into bossy mode, to trust Jean and to trust herself. It was something Lucinda Mae picked up from her dad, this sometimes bossy way of being, and Lucinda Mae didn't like it. She looked Jean in the eyes. Much was said in that look, that silence. Jean gave Lucinda Mae a peck on the cheek and headed toward her house. "Meet me, I mean, see you at Mimi's," Lucinda Mae yelled.

৵ ৲৹

As Lucinda Mae headed down the creek, her thoughts turned from Jean to Miss Cartmill. She wondered about the lives of people, how much more there was inside everyone than what you saw, even with people you knew, you loved. Seeing her teacher at church was strange for Lucinda Mae. And strange, too, for the adults there, the parents and others of Laurel Fork who did not trust the lady. If Miss Cartmill had ever attended church before yesterday, Lucinda Mae hadn't noticed it, and if she hadn't seen her, then Miss Cartmill must have been downright sneaky. Lucinda

Mae knew herself enough to know that she was as observant as she was forgetful, as if the wonders of the present stole her mind from other things. She wondered if Miss Cartmill might have been visiting church for help with her health.

It took a while to feed and water the chickens, and just as she finished, Jean hustled up to greet her. At the sight of her friend, Lucinda Mae felt like she was floating. "I went to your Mimi's but didn't see you," Jean said, "so I figured you were here."

"Let's go fetch Hoss from my Mimi," Lucinda Mae said, smiling. But then her face turned serious. "Remember, we're going squirrel hunting. Hoss is going to help us. That's all we're doing."

"That's all," Jean said. "We're just going after squirrels."

↩ ↪

The sun was bright now, but the air was still cold and the wind even gustier. Lucinda Mae saw the map in her mind as they walked a long saddle between drainages. The slope wasn't as steep nor as densely forested here as in the bottoms where little creeks tumbled like twisted shoestrings. But Painter Mountain was getting rockier the higher she and Jean climbed. With more rocks, Lucinda Mae noticed, there were fewer trees. They'd been hoofing it for over an hour. They didn't hurry and they didn't dawdle either. This was further than either of them had been, new territory. They were breathing hard, their breath visible on the cold air, and steam rose from their heads, too. Lucinda Mae's legs were tired, and she knew Jean's were tired as well, but she liked the way it all felt. She felt closer to home somehow, and she thought that was strange but maybe not that strange, like Painter Mountain was a kind of relative, like she was a member of its family.

The girls were happy to have Hoss for company. He stayed close to Lucinda Mae most of the time, but now and then he'd nose a scent and roam, though rarely was he out of sight. The sun's place in the sky said it was mid-morning. Jean was hungry again and said so to Lucinda Mae. At the end of the saddle, they found themselves at the top of a bowl-like feature in the mountain. It was the head of two drainages. The path between the trees had been large up till now, due to logging in the past, but pines grew here, grew closer together, their greenery providing some relief from the wind. Lucinda Mae and Jean sat on the ground against a log and shared banana bread.

Hoss curled snug against Lucinda Mae's hip. The girls sat in silence. Lucinda Mae understood that Jean's normal talky ways were not the same now, and she didn't fret it. She scratched Hoss behind his ears and looked around, as Jean did. The ground here was soft, too frozen to be damp. She counted six vultures soaring on the wind, which was blowing loud through the treetops. She watched the limbs bending with the gusts. The sound called to mind her flour sifter. The sun was a bit warmer now, and her body had warmed from the climb, too, and she felt strong. According to the map, they would soon encounter a flat, followed by another long climb to the top. There was an old mine in that flat. Mr. Speed had marked it with a symbol of a shovel.

She looked toward the top of Painter Mountain, but it was not visible. She looked harder but could not see any of the sky's light through the trees. Painter Mountain, even in winter with the leaves off the hardwoods, was too thickly timbered to see its top ridgeline. It was a broad mountain, not peaked like mountains out West that she'd seen in magazine photos. Painter Mountain was too old and weathered to have a sharp peak.

She looked at Hoss by her side. His head was up. He sniffed, alert. A soft growl rose in his throat. Lucinda Mae and Jean both looked around and then at each other and then looked around again. Lucinda Mae's eyes stopped on a witch hazel tree in blossom, its blossoms a deeper yellow than any dress she owned. Their shape reminded her of spiders. "What a lovely thing," she said to Jean, pointing at the small tree, "to have flowers in December." Lucinda Mae rose and directly marched to the small tree. She didn't notice that Hoss had run, tail up, in the opposite direction.

"It is pretty," Jean said. "But what's Hoss doing?"

"He's being Hoss," Lucinda Mae said, without looking back. She regarded the tree for a good while. She ran her fingers along the branches, circled the trunk, took long draughts of the blossoms' citrusy scent, and touched gently the frond-like, golden petals. She imagined having a witch hazel as a Christmas tree instead of the fir trees they cut from the farm on the north side of Laurel Fork. It was a tradition for her family to fetch a tree from the Linklet's on Christmas Eve and then to decorate it after a big dinner. Tomorrow was Christmas Eve. Lucinda Mae turned from the witch hazel and looked up the mountain. She again tried to see traces of light from the sky between the trees, but there were none, which meant they had some distance yet. "We better get on it," she told Jean.

But Hoss was gone. Lucinda Mae scanned the ground in every direction. She listened hard. The wind continued to howl on the far ridge. She heard squirrel chatter. A distant airplane. A rooster crowed far in the valley. Small birds cheeped and rustled in shrubs. She didn't hear Hoss, but she decided to trust the dog to keep up with them. Lucinda Mae never fretted too much over dogs. Dogs had proven time and again to her that they could take care of themselves and that they would find their people if their people were deserving.

"What about Hoss," Jean said.

"He'll find us," Lucinda Mae said. "He knows where we are."

The level was damp as they cut across the contour of it, damp even with the cold, the leaves fairly quiet under their steps. They studied the ground ahead and, measuring it against what they'd just crossed, decided the drainage ran just underground here before spilling along the surface again downslope. Their boots tangled in a mess of old stalks. This was thick growth, this damp ground, in warm months, and Lucinda Mae imagined wildflowers, mushrooms, salamanders, birds. Deer prints pocked the mud. There was bear scat, a seedy pile as large as Hoss' torso. (Fyce hounds are small, and Hoss smaller than most of his breed, his name a sign of her Mimi's weird sense of humor.) Where the heck was Hoss, Lucinda Mae wondered.

The flat ended. The friends navigated a boulder garden. Mossy boulders, lots of leaves that hid holes in the ground, between the rocks. The girls stepped with care. Here were ankle snappers, knee twisters, shin scrapers. Soon, they approached a boulder the size of a schoolbus. Ice hung, a frozen waterfall. A rancid smell filled their noses. Lucinda Mae stopped, one foot on a rock, the other foot on a boulder, a big hole between them. She stared at the mass of rock ahead of her. Jean stood to her side, similarly balanced.

They saw Hoss. He was at the base of the ice falls, on another mass of ice and stone where in warmer weather a pool of water would have been. Lucinda Mae called to him, but he didn't look up. He had found, Lucinda Mae and Jean saw, a dead deer, a yearling doe, and was busy rubbing against it. "Aw, so that's it," Lucinda Mae said. She called to him again, her voice more pointed, sharp. He looked up, wagged the stump of his tail, and then looked around. Lucinda Mae followed his eyes. The waterfall with its adjacent boulders and slabs reminded her of the theater at Laurel Fork High School. It was like being inside a box of stone, except one side was missing. She stared a few moments out the missing side towards the valleys and ridges from which they'd come. Hoss broke her trance with his sudden, high-pitched yapping. Lucinda Mae turned, caught the sight of a vulture coming to roost on a nearby maple's branch. Hoss stared at it and growled.

Lucinda Mae looked at Jean, and Jean must have felt her gaze, because she immediately turned. "I'm sad for the deer, but this place is amazing," Jean said.

"Sure is," Lucinda Mae said. She smiled as she looked at her friend. "I'm glad you're here with me."

"I'm happy to be here with you," Jean said, smiling. "It's a little scary, but I feel safe somehow, too."

"Me, too," Lucinda Mae said. "And let's hope Miss Cartmill will be happy we're here." Jean nodded with a concerned look. The girls continued to admire the place. Ice, stone, moss, sky, trees. There was power here, they both felt it, and both sensed that they were not the first ones to stand here and feel it. The feeling was one of holiness. They felt small and yet they also felt a great strength in that smallness.

Lucinda Mae's eyes fixed on a tangle of logs and dead leaves bundled in a mass at the base of the cliff as if a flood had deposited it. Beyond it, she noticed a strange metal object in a hollow under the boulder, a dry place. The sight sent a chill through her. "Come on, Jean," she said, "let's check something."

Jean followed. They approached the cliff, stepping with care on the icy, stony ground. The metal was clearly from an old cot, a sleeping cot. The springs were rusted. All of it was rusted. They scanned the area, which was a sort of den, dry from weather. There were tracks in the frozen dirt, some cat, a bobcat maybe. Here and there were white splotches of bird dung. A warm breeze rose from the flat by which they'd come, different from the wind that still howled through the trees.

Lucinda Mae remembered she was looking for reindeer antler, a detail that she'd either forgotten or so fully digested it was a part of her being now. She didn't fret. She knew from experience that most good

things she'd found, she'd found when she wasn't looking. This is how she found the yummy morel mushrooms in spring when the dogwood bloomed. This is
how she found feathers and arrowheads and crayfish
and heart-shaped rocks in Painter Creek.

Lucinda Mae fetched the map from her coat pocket
and studied it once more, trying again to imagine how
an antler would look half buried on winter ground. A
chunk of ice broke from the cliff and shattered as it
landed on more ice. All around, the woods were noisy
with quiet. Jean stood by her now and took Lucinda
Mae's right hand in her left one as she looked with her
at the map.

"How much further?" Jean asked.

"I think we're well over halfway," Lucinda Mae
answered.

Hoss was back at the dead deer. As the girls
approached, the little dog growled. Lucinda Mae
knew he was being possessive. They stopped a few feet
from it. The deer was not a doe as she'd thought, it
was a spike buck. But only one spike remained. They
both looked up the cliff of the bus-sized boulder. The
deer had fallen. Perhaps it had been chased. When
she looked back at the deer, Lucinda Mae noticed the
broken spike a few feet from the body.

"Okay, Hoss, he's yours," Lucinda Mae said. "But
this is mine." She reached for the ivory spike. Hoss
paid no mind. It was six inches long, with a gentle

curve, the antler. The beginning of a tine jutted from it, about an inch from its base. As she held it, Lucinda Mae imagined holding a knife with this as the handle.

"It's not a reindeer antler," Jean said, "but it's something. I feel like we're on the right track."

Lucinda Mae nodded. "Me, too," she said. "Come on, Hoss," she continued as she zipped the spike's broken antler in her knapsack. "Let's leave this be. We need to get over this rocky place."

Lucinda Mae and Jean followed Hoss around and up the edge, out of the little gorge. Breathing hard, they crested the steepest slope and found more hardwood forest, a long gradual rise of a ridge for simple walking. Hoss stayed close as Lucinda Mae and Jean chugged along.

"How are your legs doing?" Jean asked.

"Good."

"Mine are good, too," Jean said.

"I bet," Lucinda Mae said. "You have strong legs." Lucinda Mae kept her eyes at work scanning the leafy ground, and as she did so she thought of the cot under the cliff's overhang. She wondered who had slept there. It was a nice place for a den. She thought that maybe it was a miner's camp. Speed's map noted a mine somewhere around that place, but they had not seen one. They were looking for a reindeer antler, not mines.

At the top of the next rise, Lucinda Mae and Jean took another break. They sat in the day's quiet, finished the leftover meatloaf, and drank some water. Lucinda Mae realized she'd neglected to bring her rainproof pack of matches with old dryer lint for fire starter. She looked down at where her gun lay on the leaves. There was something comforting about the gun. She liked knowing it had been her father's when he was a boy and had before that been his father's gun when he was a boy. She wondered what stories that gun could tell. Sometimes she felt like she'd heard them all, though she never could have repeated them.

The sun now appeared well beyond the noon place in the sky, and Lucinda Mae then realized she'd forgotten the flashlight as well as her fire kit. She wondered, perplexed. They'd need a lot of luck to find the antler in the day's remaining light. She scanned upslope and saw sky between the trees, a sure sign that they were close to the summit. For a minute she felt a strong urge to run up there, for on the north flank of the mountain's top was likely the corral.

Soon, Hoss was nipping at her boots as she hustled the last hundred yards up the mountain. Jean stayed right with her. The wind howled hard up here. The girls had been climbing the south side, with the wind from the north, but now they felt that high-pressure cold front full in their faces. It was exhilarating.

"We made it!" Lucinda Mae said.

"Yes, we did," said Jean with a hoot as they kept walking.

Lucinda Mae hooted as well. "It's beautiful up here," she said, "and the air's wild and fresh."

"It's amazing," said Jean.

"Ama-a-a-azing," Lucinda Mae said, almost yodeled. Her gun felt heavy but she felt strong with its weight as she moved along the terrain. The ground was soft underfoot, a thin layer of snow still covering it. She kept her eyes glued to the ground, scanning back and forth. She remembered the rock slab from her Mimi's photo.

"I bet old cedar and locust posts would likely be standing where the corral had been," Jean said.

Lucinda Mae nodded. From certain places through the trees, the girls could see for miles. The view was best to the north and west. There were a few roofs visible and a lot of logging roads. The sky was endless. The ground, it looked like a giant egg crate of hills and valleys. Cliffs were visible, as was a river winding its way along a meandering path.

The wind was full on their faces. They had each worked up a little sweat while climbing the last pitch, and now they both felt a chill as the wind found its way through their clothes' seams. But they didn't stand long. Jean spotted an old locust corner-post just downslope, and pointed it out.

Hoss and Lucinda Mae followed Jean as she traversed her way down there. The going was steep down the north face. There was still an inch or so of snow over here on the north side, and it had hardened, so Lucinda Mae dug her boots in edgeways for purchase. There were animal prints in the snow, but the girls didn't have time to study them. Hoss took care of that, sniffing and growling and making yellow slush.

From the corner post, Lucinda Mae could recognize the entire corral. She noted the rock slab as well as how many trees had repopulated since that time of the old photo, when Painter Mountain had been mostly bald from the forest fire. She saw, too, how her Mimi's Uncle Roy and Mr. Speed sure had set some lasting posts way back when for the one-eyed lady. Except for a place or two, the wire had rusted and popped its fastenings.

"Find that antler!" Lucinda Mae called to Hoss. Hoss barked and leaped at her knee. The girl took the spike's antler from her knapsack and let him chew on it, but she didn't let him take it. Quickly, she put it away and as she walked circles from the outside of the corral inwards, she said to the little Fyce hound, "Get. Fetch that antler."

Jean chimed in, too. "Get that antler," Jean said. "Get it! Get it! Get it!"

It was easy with their tracks in the snow to see what ground they'd covered, and before long they'd scanned the entire corral. No antler.

Lucinda Mae felt her spirit wane, but she took a deep breath and worked to stay on task. "We can't give up," she said to Jean.

Jean was looking out over the valley. "No," Jean said as she turned to meet her friend's gaze. "We can't give up."

So they did it again, this time from the inside to the outside, to the remains of the fence. A few ferns peeked through the snow. Lucinda Mae pictured Miss Cartmill in the classroom and in her car, and she tried to see her looking healthy and well, not so ill-looking. Maybe thinking positively would bring her closer to the antler.

Here, now, were dead branches, the edges of large rocks and a few stumps. A squirrel had dug up several caches of acorns or other nuts. Again their search, and the dog's, turned up nothing.

Lucinda Mae checked the sun. The fireball burned only three finger widths above the horizon. She felt frustrated, but she knew they had to turn back. "We better get going," she said. "It's a long return trip."

"Really? But downhill will be faster," Jean said.

"The nights come fast around Christmas time," Lucinda Mae said.

"Can't we look again," Jean asked, "just one more time?"

"I want to look all night," Lucinda Mae said, with annoyance. Of course she wanted to look again. "Jean, it'd be dangerous."

"Alright," said Jean, shaking her head with disappointment.

"It's okay, Jean," Lucinda Mae said, and as she started to move back the way they'd come, she knew it didn't really feel okay to her. She just hoped saying so would make it feel better. "We're not giving up," she said to Jean as they walked. "We're just being smart. We have to be smart. Let's go."

Just as she crested the rise before their long trip down the south flanks, a deep, earthy smell filled her nose. She turned and noticed movement in a patch of laurel off the edge of the corral's western border. A few seconds later, a large bear ambled forth, nose up, sniffing.

Lucinda Mae stood still, checked for Hoss, and looked at Jean, who was standing still as an icicle. Hoss was over the rise, she hoped, when she didn't see him. It was a big bear, but there were no cubs, no cubs yet out of the laurel anyway, and Lucinda Mae was grateful for that. She knew that the girls' location was in their favor, that the bear wouldn't smell them where it stood upwind, but her heart still ran like a jackrabbit.

Then Hoss started barking. No, she realized, that wasn't Hoss. The barking was deeper, that of bear hounds, the dogs that local hunters used to tree the bear. She knew the sound well. The bear heard it, too, and galloped across the slope with surprising speed. It took off without noticing Lucinda Mae or Jean. The barking of the hounds grew louder. Lucinda Mae and Jean did not wait around to see the chase.

⊕ ⊕

Lucinda Mae had been daydreaming about Mimi's story of Red Dress, but she knew they'd made good time on the first leg of the return trip. Soon, they were back at the bus-sized boulder. She saw the sun shone still two and a half finger-widths above the horizon. "Let's have a snack," she said to Jean. Jean sat on a deadfallen tree trunk, and Lucinda Mae joined her, sharing a good portion of the venison bologna.

Between bites, Jean said, "We failed."

Lucinda Mae felt a rising sadness, but she pushed against it, "We didn't succeed," Lucinda Mae said to her friend, a little sharply. "Not that time."

"Are you saying we're coming back up here again?" Jean asked with her mouth now full of bologna.

"We have to try again," Lucinda Mae said, and gave her friend an annoyed look.

"What if we fail again?" Jean asked, still looking down at the leaves.

"Then we fail a second time," Lucinda Mae said. She knew she needed to do something. Her friend didn't go down in the dumps too often, but when she did it wasn't any fun. She held out her hand. "Jean," she said, "give me your hand."

"Will we try again then, too," Jean asked, slumping her shoulders even further, not offering her hand.

"You're starting to get under my skin," said Lucinda Mae. "Give me your hand, Jeannie Beannie."

"Sorry," Jean said, putting her left hand in Lucinda Mae's right one. "I just thought we'd find the antler."

"I thought we would find it, too," Lucinda Mae said as she threaded her fingers through her friend's and squeezed, held firm.

"Maybe we're crazy," Jean said, a little lift in her voice. "Maybe Mr. Speed's crazy, too."

"Now shush, Jean," Lucinda Mae said warmly, "please." Then she spotted Hoss. He was back at the deer corpse, rubbing and sniffing.

Lucinda Mae watched as Jean slipped her fingers out of her hand, stood and walked over to Hoss, and then around the lower flank of the giant boulder, an area that neither girl had checked out on their way up the mountain. Lucinda Mae pulled on her gloves again, flung the gun over her shoulder, and marched to join her. The air felt colder to her with the sun lower, and then she realized that the wind was blowing less rowdy now than it had all day.

Jean had stopped before a deep hole, deep and broad. "Look at this, Lucinda Mae," she said.

Lucinda Mae came up next to Jean and saw that between boulders in the bottom of the hole, there was an opening.

"This must be the mine that's on the map! The map labels it a soapstone mine. Nice work spying it."

"Soapstone," Jean said. "Miss Cartmill taught us a lesson on that in Earth Science. A soft stone, smooth to the touch. Takes well to carving."

"Yes," Lucinda Mae said, "Mr. Speed has mortar and pestles of soapstone, and my Mimi has a bowl." This was exciting. It felt good to have the reindeer antler off their mind for a bit. She felt a sudden urge to take some soapstone home, so she rested her gun carefully against her knapsack on the leaves and scrambled behind Jean into the hole.

The girls didn't notice the way Hoss stood at the rim of the pit, his stump tail down, hair up and spiky along his spine. He whined gently, quietly.

They'd left their flashlights at home, but were a good ways into the cave now, on hands and knees. The light of day no longer penetrated, and everything Lucinda Mae touched felt very unrocklike.

"This place is weird," Jean said.

The air wasn't as cold in the cave as it was outside. It felt peaceful. Lucinda Mae liked the place, but she knew they couldn't linger. She wondered what Hoss was doing. She was surprised the little hound hadn't followed them. She tried to see her hand in the dark. She was holding her hand almost to her nose when she heard something. There were voices.

"What was that," Jean asked, her voice tight.

"Quiet," Lucinda Mae said as a shiver quivered through her belly, "listen."

The girls listened.

The sounds emerged from deep in the cave and with them arose a smell like burnt lard. It was a living smell, however, and Lucinda Mae felt so suddenly and totally terrified that she screamed, and Jean screamed, too, in unison. The voices stopped then, or maybe they didn't because Lucinda Mae and Jean scrambled so fast out of that mine, and so noisily, that they wouldn't have heard them.

"Let's run," Lucinda Mae yelled, "and not stop!" She could hear Jean just behind her. She didn't check to see that Hoss was keeping up with them. She didn't even slow down when a ruckus of wild turkeys took to roost as she tromped up on them. There was nothing in her mind except getting off of that mountain and making sure Jean did, too.

6

Lucinda Mae and Jean approached the edge of the woods where the field began, and they stopped running. They were both exhausted and confused. Lucinda Mae leaned against a grizzled, old maple tree. Her legs felt like rubber bands. Hoss stood by her ankle, looking ready for more activity, the rascal. She couldn't help but smile at the little dog and then up at Jean, who'd been staring at her.

Jean smiled, shook her head. "That was nuts!"

Lucinda Mae didn't say anything. She could hear Painter Creek across the field and see Mimi's place and her own house, too. Just as she caught her breath, she remembered she'd left the gun and her knapsack at the edge of the pit. Some thunder roared through her nerves. She groaned. She closed and did not want to open her eyes.

"What's the matter?" Jean asked.

"Ugh," Lucinda Mae said.

"What?" Jean asked.

"I left the gun and knapsack. My dad's gun." Lucinda Mae said, eyes open again. She spotted activity at the hog pen that occupied a place at the edge of her parent's six acres. Mr. Hall's big red pickup was parked there. She could hear voices. Half the sun still poked over the ridge to the southwest. The light was a mix of violet and gold and would have been soothing were the girl in the market for being soothed. Her head started to ache, first at the right temple and then across to the left.

"I'm so sorry," Jean said. "But at least we got out of there." There was a pause. Jean walked up to her and took her hand. "We know where the gun and knapsack are. We'll get them."

Lucinda Mae looked from the hog pen to her friend and smiled sadly.

"You need a bear hug," Jean said as she squeezed her with all she had. Lucinda Mae forgot the pain in her ankle. She felt moved by her friend's kindness and bravery. She heard her dad's voice then and saw that Mr. Hall and her father were loading the hogs for the butcher. "It's too late to return for the gun and knapsack," Jean said.

"Not without a flashlight anyway," said Lucinda Mae.

"Even with a light," Jean said, "those voices in the cave, they were just too spooky."

Lucinda Mae said, "I'm in a pickle."

Jean smiled at Lucinda Mae using her Mimi's words. "We're both in a pickle," Jean said. "We're in this together."

Lucinda Mae felt herself start to cry a little, the tears a mix of frustration and gratitude. Jean hugged her again. "We're lucky," Jean said. "We have an excuse to go back up there."

Lucinda Mae looked at Hoss again and tried to smile even as she felt the storm hardening to a lump in her chest. "You're right. We have a really good excuse. We can't stop trying to help Miss Cartmill. But we need a story, too."

"I've got that," Jean said. "I mean, we'll blame it on the bear. We can say the bear charged us."

"Yes!" Lucinda Mae nearly shouted. "We can't give up."

"True," said Jean.

"True, true, true," said Lucinda Mae. "And let's say it happened, that the bear charged us up on that second pitch, that the gun is at the laurel patch where we had a snack."

"Okay," said Jean. "That's smart."

"Or it's saucy," Lucinda Mae said, smiling.

Jean looked up from her watch with a worried face. "Cinda, I have to get home. There's this stuff with my uncle and all."

"I understand," Lucinda Mae said. She wished her friend could stay for dinner, at least, but she knew it wasn't possible.

↩ ↪

The warmth on Mimi's face shifted to a more serious look as she took in the sight of her granddaughter on the front stoop. Lucinda Mae, feeling downcast, shook her head, and then she looked up, stared low in the sky where the sun was a sliver. The light was going from violet to hot pink now.

"Mimi," she muttered. She was still looking at the sky. "I'm in a pickle."

"Come in here, girl, and let's talk it over."

Hoss was already inside Mimi's place. When the two entered, he was eating from his dog bowl, crunching the dry food with great speed. Lucinda Mae plopped on the sofa, but she stood again almost immediately. She felt restless.

"You get any squirrels?" her Mimi asked.

"Yes, one early in the morning."

"Good," her Mimi said. "What's on your mind?"

Lucinda Mae told a false story of her day on the mountain. It wasn't easy to do this. She was dying to tell her Mimi the truth. Mimi probably would have kept it a secret, but Lucinda Mae just wasn't sure; her grandmother was hard to predict. She couldn't risk the grown-ups putting a stop to their plan. She and Jean, they had to keep looking for the antler.

"Pickle's the right word for it," Mimi said when she was quiet again.

"What should I do?" Lucinda Mae started. "I'm thinking of going after the gun now. I could get up there in an hour or so. There might be enough moonlight."

"Forget the gun and your bag," Mimi said. "Get home first and check in with your parents. They're so busy with Peanut, and your dad with the mail work, and Christmas, they won't ask."

"Okay," Lucinda Mae said after a while. Her voice was softer, tired. "That's what I'll do."

❧ ❧

Mr. Hall and Mr. Coggins had busted down the barrier that allowed the hogs into the corral where the red pickup was parked, its gate down. Mr. Hall stood in the bed with clabbered milk and crushed corn to lure the two big animals. Lucinda Mae had fed her hens and fetched the eggs in a basket, and now she paused by the fence, watching her dad shuffle alongside the hogs.

He held the octagonal panel of an old, faded stop sign in front of him, as a barrier. The two hogs bucked and sprinted and then stood or walked. Mr. Hall called to them in a syrupy, loud voice. "Hee-hawr," he shouted. "Hee-hawr, hee-hawr-hawg." They looked hungry. Tension oozed from all involved, a little cloud of it condensing over the corral.

One hog started for the truck, and Mr. Coggins scurried behind the more tentative one, bumping it with the old stop sign. It always surprised Lucinda Mae how fast the large, long animals were. Now both pigs approached the truck. Mr. Hall tossed a bit of corn their way and they snorted. One, the largest of the hogs, foamed at the mouth. Mr. Coggins trotted up. Lucinda Mae saw that her father was concentrating hard. This was serious work. The animals were over three hundred pounds each, and her family had spent a lot of time and money feeding them. They would provide many meals as well as some income from the cuts they sold. But so was looking for the antler serious work, she reminded herself, so too was trying to help Miss Cartmill.

Lucinda Mae kept watching her father. Something about his face annoyed her, she realized after a moment. It was the same face, grim and determined, that he wore when he got after her for being sloppy or forgetful. It was the same face her mom called his Vietnam face, when they bickered, which wasn't too often. She knew her dad had been for a year in Vietnam, but he never talked about it. She liked to see his olive green coat and shirt with the patches on it, but she didn't feel ready to ask him about it yet. She knew from her mom that it was a heavy subject for him.

Lucinda Mae's father caught her eyes. He nodded to her silently to come through the fence and lend a hand. She wondered if he could sense her mishap with the gun. Mr. Hall saw their exchange and nodded in agreement. Mr. Hall was a big man, and his face was hot, nearly as red as his truck. Steam rose from his head. Especially next to her dad, who was strong in a wiry, ropy way, and not very tall, Mr. Hall looked huge.

The light was fading fast now. Lucinda Mae climbed the fence with care—her ankle felt sore from the run down the mountain; not injured, just a stinger—and entered the corral. The hogs pretended not to see her. She approached slowly and tried to act calm, like everything was fine. Her father handed her the old stop sign with a quiet, "Thanks, Cinda."

It took nearly to pitch dark before they had the hogs in the truck bed, a wooden gate fitted high around it. Now Lucinda Mae climbed from the rear tire to the gate and tossed hay from a square bale her father held. The hogs were starting to settle down. The air smelled like hay and hog waste and the sun-drained air of night.

"I sure appreciate it," Mr. Coggins said to Mr. Hall.

"Glad to help," Mr. Hall responded.

"Let me run you home then," Mr. Coggins said.

"It's that time," said Mr. Hall. "They'll be fine tonight."

"I hope so," Mr. Coggins said. "You heard one of Bryant Deacon's calves got mauled last night. A bad moon . . . they say it wasn't coyotes either."

"Then what they reckon was it?" Mr. Hall asked.

"They're saying painter."

Lucinda Mae saw Mr. Hall shake his head. After a time, he said, "I'll be."

↜ ↝

Lucinda Mae found her mama nursing Peanut in the living room. She looked contented. Music came from the radio. The volume was low, but Lucinda Mae could make out a lady with a pretty voice singing and playing dulcimer. It was a Christmas song.

"About time," Mrs. Coggins said to her daughter in a sweet way.

"A big day, Mom. But just one squirrel." Lucinda Mae wanted to hold her brother. She wanted to snuggle him up. He was still having his milk.

"One's better than none. There are seven others still in the freezer." Her mother smiled and then continued, "You get it skinned up and all clean now."

"Yes, ma'am," Lucinda Mae said. She felt her vest. The animal was still in her game pocket. She went back outside. A moment later, she came back in and flipped on the switch for the shed light. And then she went back out again.

The night was young. The wind had stopped. There was hardly a breeze. Lots of stars salted the sky. The moon, a day past full, would be up before long. Lucinda Mae's knife was sharp. As she skinned and cleaned the squirrel, another Christmas song from the radio came to her lips, and she hummed it quietly while she worked.

Lucinda Mae's dad hadn't returned from taking Mr. Hall home. Back in the mudroom, the girl packed the squirrel meat and found room for it in the chest freezer. Her parents had eaten earlier, and they'd left her a plate on the woodstove. Ham and biscuits with apple butter, pickled okra and sweet potato on the side. Lucinda Mae was excited to sit for a meal, but as she washed up she noticed something that startled and stopped her. Her fingernails, all of them, were sky blue.

She looked again at her hands. She looked more closely, scratched at the index nail of the left hand with index nail of the right. This wasn't paint. The color seemed to come from under the nail. It was a rich color, pretty. "What the heck," Lucinda Mae said aloud. This was freaky. This was worse than freaky. She was nervous with wonder and worry. The gun, and now this.

"Won't you come in here to eat?" her mama called from the living room.

"Oh, Ma, I'm not so hungry. I'll take a little something outside," Lucinda Mae said. "Dad wants me to feed the hogs before he's back."

"You sound a little jumpy, Cinda," her mom said. "You okay?"

"Sure, Ma."

"Cinda," her Ma called back. "Jean called earlier. I almost forgot."

"She did?"

"Yes."

"Great," Lucinda Mae said. She paused a while by the sink and then scrubbed her nails one more time with hot water and soap. Nothing changed. She told herself that she'd found some nail polish on the side of the road. Lucinda Mae hated to lie. "Mama?"

"Yes."

"I'm going to read to the hogs again this year."

"But you've had such a big day," her mom said. There was a pause. Peanut made some funny noises. He always made funny noises after nursing. "You know, I don't hold with your dad's claim that reading to the hogs makes the meat more flavorful, but he swears by it."

"I like to do it," Lucinda Mae said.

"Well, don't be long," her mom said. "You're not reading them *Gone with the Wind*, I hope."

Lucinda Mae took the back hall to her room to fetch a book. She hadn't really heard what her mom said. She needed to keep moving; she didn't want to risk her mother seeing her nails. That would just be too much for one day, and though she needed to call Jean on the telephone, she needed to get outside for a bit.

The rising moon shone through the trees along Painter Mountain's long east flank. By the moon's glow, and by the house light that leaked from the windows, she saw the thermometer on the tree recording thirty, warmer than it had been at noon. It wasn't bright enough to make out the words in her storybook, but Lucinda Mae hadn't forgotten her flashlight this time.

She fed the hogs. Hoss showed up. Mimi must have let him out for his evening romp. But he was acting in a strange way. He rubbed against Lucinda Mae's ankles and whined. Lucinda Mae gave him some loving, scratching behind his ears and along his chest. He continued to whine and hanker for attention. "You can listen too," the girl said as she tucked her flashlight in her yellow hat, its metal cold against her head at first, its beam on the pages as she began to read.

The book was *Goodnight Moon*. It had been her favorite book when she was younger. It was easy to read, and she was reading it a little too fast before its rhythm and repetition slowed her down. The hogs lay flush to one another on the hay in the truck's bed as she read. The story eased Lucinda Mae of her worries for a little while, and she hoped that if the big pigs had worries, worries like Miss Cartmill did, the gentle words were helping them too.

When Lucinda Mae returned from her time with the pigs, her mother was seated at the kitchen table with a serious look on her face. "Did you see your dad out there?"

"No ma'am. He's not back yet." Lucinda Mae looked at her hands, the grey gloves she was still wearing.

"Cinda, you seem funny tonight. Everything okay?"

"Sure . . . yes, ma'am."

"Where did you hunt?"

"Jean and me hunted around the usual places Dad and I go."

"I'm glad Jean's back and found you, glad her uncle's doing better. Did you shoot more than once?"

"No, just one time."

"Cinda, I hope you're not getting sick. There's been a bug going around."

"I feel fine." Lucinda Mae had been standing very still by the door. A big part of her wanted to tell her mother the truth of her day, but she didn't do it and she didn't feel good about that. She moved to the counter now and without thinking, slid a plate from a bowl where it served as a lid. "You soaked tapioca, Ma," Lucinda Mae said. She was looking in the bowl. "You mind if I pudding it up."

"That'd be great," her mother said. "Your aunt came by with milk around lunchtime. Her Jersey's giving well these days."

"Perfect," Lucinda Mae said.

"And I was thinking," her mom continued. "That if you need any help with Christmas presents—I know how you always like to make them for everybody—just let me know what supplies you need. I'll be running to town tomorrow. I can pick them up then."

"Thanks, Ma," Lucinda Mae said after a minute. She was draining the water from the swollen tapioca. "But I've got everything I need."

"Are your hands cold?" her mother asked. "Why are you still wearing your gloves?"

Lucinda Mae stared in the colander. "Yes, they're still cold."

"Well, run them under the hot water a bit. They'll warm up."

She listened to her mother go down the hall. After a minute, she peeled the gloves from her hands. The nails were the same. Blue. What a doggone day. She quickly dialed Jean's number on the telephone. Luckily, Jean answered. Neither girl could speak in full voice, and they had to keep it short, but they compared notes, and sure enough they each had the same blue fingernails, and sure enough they felt a little relief in sharing their strange plight.

"Are you going to join me tomorrow?" Lucinda Mae asked.

"Yes as can be," Jean said.

"We're just going to have to see how it goes in the

morning. You come over when you can. I'm sure my mom will have lots for me to do."

"You better wait for me," Jean said.

"I'll wait for you, Jeanie Beanie," Lucinda Mae said. "No way I'm going up without you."

After the call, Lucinda Mae got busy with the tapioca. It always soothed her to cook, took her mind off what worries. Tapioca was curious stuff. She knew from reading the package that it came from the cassava, that it was a product of Brazil, but she wasn't sure if these were berries or seeds or what. She wondered if they grew anywhere near where the one-eyed lady had lost her eyes and met the monkey. The tapioca was sort of gross and pretty looking at the same time, like fish eyeballs, she thought, but it sure tasted good once cooked.

While the milk heated, she separated the whites from the yolks of two eggs. She was proud to see the deep orange color of the yolks. They reminded her of a brilliant sunrise. She had the sudden idea that if you could get cassava from Brazil, then you could probably get reindeer antler from the far north. She decided that down the line, when all this was done, she'd ask Mr. Speed if this was so.

She didn't want the milk too hot, so before she could beat the sugar with the yolks, she added the tapioca and a good pinch of salt to the double boiler, and then she covered it and let it cook on low. In an hour, she'd add the yolk-sugar mix, stirring it in. Lastly, she'd fold in the egg whites and stir in the teaspoon of vanilla. She knew the recipe by heart. There was a faster way to make it, as her Aunt Janet had showed her, but Lucinda Mae preferred the slow way. It was one of her favorite desserts, especially in winter. She'd tried it with chocolate chips, but it wasn't the same. She liked that her mother and father were fond of the simple dessert too.

Lucinda Mae washed dishes while the mixture cooked. Meanwhile, she cooked up a plan. She was running it through her mind again when her father returned from delivering Mr. Hall. The girl made sure she kept her hands under the water.

"Hey, Lucinda Mae."

"Hi, Dad."

"Thanks for your help with the hogs," he said. He sounded worn out. "It's always a trick getting them in the truck."

"Sure. It's nice of Mr. Hall to lend us his truck." Lucinda Mae wiped her hands on a dish towel. It was the faded blue towel with rooster designs and a heart-shaped skillet stain. She kept wiping them, hiding her fingers in its folds.

"We'll thank him with fresh sausage," her dad said. "How was your day?"

"It was a good day." Lucinda Mae felt her stomach drop. She wanted to tell him the whole story, the truth. She wasn't good at fibbing. "I'm making tapioca pudding."

"Count me in for a bowl of that," her dad said. "Is your mama with Peanut?"

"I think so."

⊰ ⊱

Much to her parents' amusement, Lucinda Mae wore the white gloves from her dress-up clothes chest as they sat at the table, enjoying the warm dessert. She hadn't played dress-up in a long time. But after the initial funny part, neither her mother nor her father paid much attention to her gloved hands. Peanut was fussy, and they were busy finalizing this year's Christmas plans.

Mr. Coggins had to work on Christmas Eve. After chores, Aunt Janet would come over for dinner and then afterwards hang ornaments and sing carols around the tree. Lucinda Mae wished she was more excited about Christmas, but as she ate she came to see that the celebration would be different this year. So be it. If anything, there was more excitement, just of a different sort. She told herself to keep on. She had a job to do. She had a teacher who was sick and needed help and she had a great friend helping her, too. She trusted that Jean and she would figure out a way.

The day was coming to a close. Mr. Coggins washed up the dishes after dessert. Lucinda Mae went to bed, but she couldn't sleep. Her mind was racing. She tossed and turned. The moonlight gave the world outside her window a bluish glow. She watched as one of the cats from down the road, the tabby one, skulked along the fence. It was a little after nine, according to her clock.

At ten, not having slept a wink, Lucinda Mae rose from bed and dressed in the same clothes she'd worn that day. She packed her flashlight in her knapsack, opened her window, slid up the pane on the storm, and squeezed through the opening after tossing out the knapsack. There was a slight drop to the ground. She landed it with ease.

She stood a moment. She wasn't thinking, she was feeling. She fetched a stepladder from the tool shed and used it to get the height needed to close the window again. Then she stopped. She stood on the ladder outside her bedroom window. The night was inviting, not too cold. But Lucinda Mae was frozen in thought. She had never snuck out of her room before now.

She stood there, three rungs from the top of the ladder. What am I doing out here? she wondered. You're getting some air, she told herself. And you're clearing your head. You're feeling guilty for not telling your parents about what you're doing. She kept on telling herself things. But you can't tell them because Miss Cartmill needs you, she's sick and she needs you and Jean to find the antler, and if you tell them they'll think it's crazy and dangerous and who knows what all, and they'll never let you go squirrel hunting or maybe even to school ever again. She looked at her blue fingernails by the light of the moon. After a while, she climbed back in her bedroom and shut the window behind her.

She didn't go to her parents. She lay in her bed, and felt much sleepier than before. She could hardly keep her eyes open with the house warm and cozy with the creamy vanilla smell of tapioca. She felt her yellow nightgown on her skin, her soft, yellow pillow folded in half under her head just like she liked it. She hoped Jean was comfortable in bed too.

7

Lucinda Mae slept hard. Her alarm woke her at five. As she washed up and dressed, fragments of the night's dream came to her. She had been wearing a crown of honeysuckle vine, its leaves frozen, though she hadn't felt the cold. There were many people watching her in the dream. She couldn't place who they were, but they were familiar and friendly. She didn't remember what else she wore, but she was in a kitchen, some kitchen that didn't seem like her own. There were trees in this kitchen, whether winter or summer trees, she didn't know. She had been trying to grind flour with a hand crank mill much like the one her father had given her mother years ago for Christmas. But every way she'd turned the handle, she cranked it the wrong direction. No flour could be made. She had turned and turned the handle, with no feelings of frustration, no feelings at all, as the wheat berries remained in the little hopper, unwilling to become flour.

"Good morning," her father said. He was standing at the stove, a smell of oatmeal in the air when Lucinda Mae entered the kitchen.

"Hi, Dad." Lucinda Mae felt her mother's footsteps through the floorboards. And she heard a sneeze and then the blowing of a nose. Her father looked cheerful but tired. He had a small red spot on his chin where he'd cut himself shaving.

"Mama okay?" Lucinda Mac asked.

"She's got a little cold. Didn't sleep much. Baby was up a bunch."

"I hope she'll rest some more, then."

"That's her plan," her father said. "I've taken her some tea."

Lucinda Mae glanced out the window, saw Mr. Hall's red truck in the corral. The hogs were not visible, still bedded on the hay. "What'd your thermometer read?" her dad asked.

"Still thirty degrees."

"That's good. Not too cold."

"I wonder if it will stay or rise today."

"The guy on the radio said mid-forties, but that's Greenville. Warmer there." Her father stopped. He looked at Lucinda Mae. "You paint your fingernails?"

Lucinda Mae held up her hand. They were chapped with winter weather and work, and that the blue had paled to a hue like the color of Painter Mountain certain summer days. "I forgot," she said. "A while ago. They're fading now."

"Strange," her dad said, and Lucinda Mae felt nervous for a moment, though she knew he was too busy to focus on it. He needed to get to work.

"Any snow?" Lucinda Mae asked. She had fetched a kettle from the woodstove and poured them both a mug of tea. The cream from her Aunt Janet's Jersey made the liquid turn the color of the creek after a hard rain. She remembered the tapioca she'd made from the skim. There was a good bit of pudding left over, and it had surely firmed up by now.

"A chance of rain and freezing rain starting around noon," her dad said.

Lucinda Mae was itching for her and Jean to have a plan for the day, but she also enjoyed the slow ritual of early morning with her father. She liked to see him in his work clothes, fixing oatmeal the same way he did each day, with lots of butter and a palmful of frozen blueberries from their summer pickings off the patch of highbush they grew.

Her father sat with her at the table. He took a bite, chewed, swallowed. "I'll be running these hogs to the Grant's shop and then work until four. We'll have Mr. Linklet deliver a tree today." He took another bite. Lucinda Mae sensed that he had more to say. The oatmeal tasted a bit thicker than usual. Lucinda Mae worried he might ask about the gun.

"We're not cutting it ourselves this year?" Lucinda Mae asked. Disappointing.

"Not this year, I'm sorry to say," her dad said. "Too much going on."

"I understand," said Lucinda Mae, and for a moment she hated the postal service for stealing her dad all the time.

"Did you clean the gun yet?" her dad asked, as if on cue.

Lucinda Mae grimaced a little. "Not yet. Jean and I are going back out today."

"Oh, good," her dad said. He ate more oatmeal. Lucinda Mae thought she heard Peanut making nursing sounds.

"With the weather as it is, and the days so short, I want you to let your mama know when you and Jean go, and you'll take the walkie-talkie too, leaving the other with her. Their batteries are charged." He nodded to the counter by the telephone. "See them there?"

"I do," Lucinda Mae said. "But, Dad, these things are heavy. I don't like them."

"It's not up for discussion," he said as he stood. His voice sounded weary. "I have to run. Let me give you a hug." Lucinda Mae stood up from the table. Her father was not normally one for giving hugs. This felt a little funny until she felt his warmth.

"Dad, thanks again for letting me squirrel hunt."

"You're very welcome."

"Dad . . ." she said again before he shut the door to go.

"Yes."

"Have a great day."

"I will," he said. "You, too." She stared at the door as it closed where he'd stood.

Lucinda Mae glanced at her fingernails as she walked down the hall, carrying her mother a bowl of oatmeal. They were faded even more, each like a sky going cloudy, a chance of snow or rain. She was surprised to feel a little disappointment. She had liked the deep, sky-blue color.

"Lucinda Mae," her mother rasped. She was trying to sound good, but her throat was scratchy, her voice dim. Peanut slept curled against her side. Lucinda Mae noticed her mom's puffy, red eyes. She spoke quietly.

"Good morning, Mom. You hungry?"

"I'd like to put something in my belly."

Lucinda Mae crawled into bed and snuggled Peanut while her mother took a few small bites of the oatmeal. "Mama," she said.

"Yes."

"Do you know Mr. Speed at all?"

Lucinda Mae saw her mom's left eyebrow raise. "I do, or used to know him."

Lucinda Mae was surprised to hear this. She tried to picture her mom as a younger woman and Mr. Speed as a younger man, and doing so made her smile. She wondered, though, what sort of connection they had, Mr. Speed and her mom. Peanut opened his eyes for a moment. He didn't blink. He was soon asleep again.

"When I was eleven," her mother began. "I've never told you this. I did a favor for Mr. Speed. Two favors. One in the spring and one in the fall." Her mother's voice loosened up, as if it benefited from her talking. "That spring he sent me to a place down in Painter Creek Gorge. You know where the reservoir is now. There was a chestnut tree down there, one of the only still keeping on. The rest of the chestnuts were downed by the blight." Lucinda Mae had heard of the chestnuts from Mimi. Mimi often referred to the big old trees, how the forest was so much different when they still grew. Her Mimi had a hutch made of chestnut, and she was proud of it.

"He wanted me to bring him a little chestnut bark," her mom went on, "so I went down there with an old friend, Sally Garland. She moved away when she married. Sally was a good friend. Speed didn't tell me who the bark was for, but he said it was for making medicine. Sally and me, we took the little map he made and found that tree and brought him some bark we trimmed with a hatchet. That gorge was some kind of place."

Lucinda Mae imagined her mother at eleven in the deep woods. She saw in her mom's eyes, their intent and sparkle, how powerful the memory was. "Mama, how come you never told me that?"

"You never asked, I suppose. Been busy with the Peanut man, too. You know."

"What about in the fall?"

"The fall he sent me for mushrooms. It was a damp fall. Painter Creek ran nearly to the bridge for weeks. Sloppy getting around, that was. Mushrooms everywhere. Except I kept bringing him back the wrong mushrooms. There were so many." Her mother's voice wrapped Lucinda Mae like a warm bath. Mrs. Coggins was deep in the memory. "Finally, after about six tries, I brought back the right mushroom, a pretty thing, purple cap, purple like those good plums Aunt Janet grows, that jam she makes."

"Wow," Lucinda Mae said after a while.

"Why do you ask?" her mom said.

Peanut was awake now. He was in a happy way, reaching for Lucinda Mae's hair and smiling, giggling some. "It's a lot of things coming together," Lucinda Mae said.

"I guess so," her mama said.

"Sometimes it feels like I'm an ingredient in some

recipe," Lucinda Mae said after a while. Her voice was light with the laughter Peanut sparked in her.

"That's one way of seeing it," her mom said. There was a pause. They looked at Peanut. Eventually, her mother asked, "What's your plan for today? You're not getting sick, are you?"

"No, I feel good, and I'm going to call Jean soon, and we're going after squirrels again."

"And Hoss too?" her mom asked.

"Yes," Lucinda Mae said. "And I better get on them."

⊰ ⊱

The ground was even softer with the thaw. Lucinda Mae liked the feel of it under her boots as she walked to the hen house. The air was comfortable. She didn't wear her yellow wool hat; her hair was enough warmth. The breeze was light, out of the south, a trace of moisture in the air. Fluffy clouds moved fast over the ridges. She fed and watered her hens, giving them a treat of leftover oatmeal. Now that the hogs were gone, scraps went to the hens again.

As Lucinda Mae latched the fence, she noticed in the mud a strange print among the other prints, a fresher print than the others. It was sizeable as a large dog's but without claw marks. She followed it. The path took her around the hen's yard and out around the corral. She lost the prints a few times but found them again. Eventually, she was standing where Mr. Hall's truck had been. What the heck, she wondered.

"Cinda," her mother rasped when she entered the house from the mudroom.

"Yes."

"Come hang on to Peanut while I shower, would you please?"

Lucinda Mae glanced at the clock on the stove. Just a little while and she could call Jean.

"But before that," her mom said. "Pull all the squirrel meat from the chest freezer. We'll have squirrel pot pie for Christmas Eve dinner. Maybe you'll bring some more for us."

Lucinda Mae did as she was told. She half hoped her mother would let her cook dinner tonight, but then she remembered how much else was going on. She imagined the corn and green beans and mashed potatoes. The blueberry pie. Her Aunt Janet would bring fresh-churned ice cream like she did every year. Last year she'd added cinnamon and maple syrup, and it was good, but Lucinda Mae preferred it just straight vanilla. She had canned some ginger pears with Jean one hot August day, and they would taste plenty scrumptious on fresh-churned vanilla ice cream.

"Should I grind some flour?" Lucinda Mae asked as she took Peanut from the bed.

"For the pot pie," her mom said as she made her way to the bathroom. "That'd be a big help."

Lucinda Mae thought about Christmas as she turned the crank on the grain grinder. She had started gifts after Thanksgiving, had made her mom and Aunt Janet each two pot holders, and for Mimi she had picked up a crossword puzzle book as well as made her a custom crossword puzzle with the words and clues being things in their life—hog, chicken, Painter Mountain, Hoss, checkers, Peanut, David, and so on. For Peanut she'd made a mobile to hang over his crib, cut outs of animals hanging by fishing line from a clothes hanger. And for Jean she'd drawn a picture of the two of them standing in Painter Creek in summertime. She'd drawn the picture on freezer paper, the outer side, and had added color with oil paints, and then used the freezer paper to wrap for Jean a good-sized log of venison bologna. But she had not yet figured out what to do for her dad. She had hammered the husks from walnuts she'd gathered from the tree across the road, but she hadn't yet cracked the nuts out from inside them. She wanted to do something more than a bag of walnuts. At the very least, she needed to recover the .20 gauge.

When her right arm tired, Lucinda Mae shifted position and ground the grain with her left. The sound of the stones rubbing together pleased her. She noticed that the nails on her left hand had faded even more since earlier, just like those on her right. The kitchen still smelled of the vanilla in the tapioca, but now there was the oatmeal smell, and the melted butter and blue-berry, too. Lucinda Mae stopped grinding and worked the flour from the tray into a measuring cup. She had ground more than she'd planned. Her arms were tired. Three cups would be plenty for drop biscuits on the pot pie.

She scrambled fast, nearly tripped on a chair leg when the phone rang. "Hello. Hey ... just get over here, if you can," Lucinda Mae said, feeling the urgency in her voice as she listened to Jean. " ... Okay ... Yes, yes ... I'll be here ... Good ... Okay, bye."

⊰ ⊱

Lucinda Mae was playing with Peanut when Jean showed up. Jean kept shaking her head and pacing the kitchen and talking, talking, talking. She stopped eating the tapioca after only one bite. She normally wolfed her food down. Mr. Coggins liked to kid her when she ate with them. "You must have parasites, girl," he'd say to Jean. And Jean'd say, "Big as parasites can be." Everybody would laugh.

"I'm ready," Jean said. "My aunt and uncle let me open a present early. It's a flashlight. Arlen got one, too. I borrowed Arlen's. We'll bring them along. They're really bright. They're the kind the police use, I think, and they're red, and big, and they take big batteries—"

"Okay!" Lucinda Mae said with a chuckle, gently cutting off her excited friend.

Lucinda Mae stowed her flashlight in the pocket of her orange vest. She dropped in her drybox of matches and dryer lint too. She wasn't nearly as bundled up as she'd been the previous day. Nor was Jean. Jean had a little backpack with her gear in it. It was sunny. The thermometer out her window read forty-two degrees. Jean said she'd stay there, by the thermometer, not risk saying too much to Mimi. Lucinda Mae agreed that was a smart thing to do.

"I'll tell you what," her Mimi said as Lucinda Mae entered the home. "That little Hoss made a real ruckus last night. I didn't sleep hardly a wink."

"Was he having nightmares?"

"No, he was up on the sofa, barking out the window."

Lucinda Mae could tell by the scent in the mobile home that her Mimi had made frog in a hole. She touched the skillet on the burner. It was still hot. And then she wandered to the hutch, looked closely at the grain of the chestnut from which it was made. There were many little holes, like pin holes.

"Wormy," said her Mimi. "Wormy chestnut." She said this every time Lucinda Mae admired the hutch.

"I saw some weird tracks out there this morning while doing my hens, Mimi. Big tracks. Looked like cat, but they were too big."

"Your hens all there?"

"They were, I think," Lucinda Mae said. "Should have counted. But the door to the hen house was closed, latched."

Lucinda Mae sensed a noise outside.

"What's that?" her Mimi asked. The girl opened the door. She saw the truck from Linklet's tree farm, a good sized fir in the bed. The Linklets did a good business trucking trees to sell in Greenville and other big places around the state. They had rows and rows of trees growing on mountainsides all over the other side of Laurel Fork. They had a boy, Doug Linklet. He was a couple of grades above her, always wore a baseball cap backwards, its bill curled just so. Lucinda Mae loved it when Jean referred to him as Mr. Pileated for the way he wore that hat.

"It's the Christmas tree," Lucinda Mae said. She tried not to sound disappointed. "Dad had it delivered this year, what with all the stuff going on."

"Oh. Look at that," Mimi said.

"I'm going to help bring the tree in. Mom's not feeling so well today."

"Shoot," Mimi said. "What she got?"

"Seems like a cold."

"Peanut okay?"

"Seems to be," Lucinda Mae said as she went to leave through the door.

"Good luck today, Cinda," her Mimi said.

The girl crossed the way with Hoss at her heels. The

place felt emptier with the hogs gone. Jean met up with her and Hoss. She had an excited look in her eyes, which made Lucinda Mae feel even more excited walking next to her now. Meanwhile, the small dog trotted a little ahead of them, purposeful.

"I think he knows we're going back up the mountain," Jean whispered.

Lucinda Mae smiled. "It won't be long now," she said to both the dog and her best friend. "We'll talk about it more when we're up in the woods."

Mrs. Coggins was at the mudroom door, telling the man from Linklet's to drop the tree in the shade by the pump house. Lucinda Mae stood off to the side, staring at the sun with her eyes closed, feeling it's warmth on her cheeks before another cloud could cover it. Hoss, in the meantime, laid streaks on every tire of the truck.

"Cinda," her mother said. "Would you run up to the attic and fetch the Christmas tree stand?"

"Yes," Lucinda Mae said, though she wanted to say 'no'. She was more than ready to start up the mountain.

"It ought to be in the back, by the fan," her mom said. "And hello, Jean."

"Okay," said Lucinda Mae.

"Hello, Mrs. Coggins," Jean said, and then continued. "Cinda, I'll wait out here."

The attic was crowded. Lucinda Mae stepped around piles and boxes. She had to bend over low so as to keep from bonking her head on the roof timbers. Nails poked through the purloins. She remembered sneaking up here during games of hide and seek with Jean. Then, like now, she liked to imagine the people assembling the roof years ago, one piece of wood, one cut, one nail at a time.

It took some rooting around to find the stand. In the process, she discovered a box labeled Uncle Roy. She saw the magic marker script on it was of her Mimi's hand. She opened it. Inside were medals from his time in the military. There were certificates and many, many photographs. The first one she noticed was of her Uncle Roy as a very young man, wearing Army clothes on a beach. He had a helmet on, and his companions were all dressed the same and wearing the same kind of smile, a smile on which bravery and fear seemed to be duking it out. Lucinda Mae wanted to spend more time with the faces and places he'd captured with his camera, but this was not the day. This was the day for Mimi's photo, the antler, Miss Cartmill, and the gun, too. Still, after a brief glance through them, after seeing the faces of her relatives and the places they visited, she felt as though her life was more broad and beautiful and strange. It all seemed a crazy quilt, and like people in general, not just her family, were much more connected than they appeared at first, and also more complicated, mysterious, and wild. She had the thought that people were like mountains. That like

Painter Mountain, people had caves, caves with minerals that made changes, animals whose antlers could nourish, plants that could do the same. As she carried the stand back downstairs to her mother, she felt a deep strength. She felt very at home. But she knew, also, that none of these feelings would help her today. They needed luck, lots of luck.

Mrs. Coggins was sitting with Jean at the kitchen table when Lucinda Mae returned with the stand. Peanut hung, drooly and cute, from the crook of his mother's arm.

"Good stuff," Jean said after swallowing. Lucinda Mae smiled.

"You can place that in the mudroom," Mrs. Coggins said to her daughter.

"Okay," she said.

"Thanks," said her mom.

"Mama, we ought to be getting on," Lucinda Mae said as she returned. She heard the impatience in her voice. She had put the stand in the far corner of the mudroom, out of the way of traffic.

"I hear you," her mom said. Lucinda Mae noticed again that Jean had worn her favorite, rattiest blue jeans, the ones she claimed brought good luck. Her mom was rocking Peanut. "Have a good time, and be safe. And, listen, you all be back by three. I saw Jean's wearing a watch. And bring us some more squirrel."

"Yes, ma'am," Lucinda Mae said with a smile. She gave her mom a kiss on the forehead and did the same for Peanut and then she grabbed the walkie-talkie from the counter.

"Channel Two," she said to her mother.

"Channel Two," her mom returned with a grin. "Over and out."

Lucinda Mae was smiling as she walked out the door. She smiled even though deep down she was nervous and felt like there were some sugared up kids playing hide and seek all through her body.

8

U p in the woods beyond the field, the girls laid out their plan, which was this: Look for reindeer antler. Believe in the antler. Trust that you're going to find it. The antler could be anywhere on the mountain, and we're going to find it because we know we are and because we're going to look all over. And we're not going to forget about the gun and the knapsack because the gun and the knapsack are going to be there, too, right where we left them!

Lucinda Mae set a steady pace as they started up Painter Mountain. According to Jean's watch, it was nearly ten. Hoss ran his regular path, covering twice the distance of the girls, circling and traversing. They stopped now and then to sip from water bottles and to shed layers of clothes, tying them around their waists. The sun shone hard on the saddle where they walked, and Lucinda Mae could see by the upturned leaves where they'd walked the prior day, and where they'd run down the mountain, too. It was warm for Christmas Eve, but such warmth wasn't especially unusual anymore.

They were making good time. Lucinda Mae's ankle felt strong. Her legs, which had been a little sore in the morning, were no longer achy. She noticed the witch hazel tree she'd admired. It brought to mind Miss Cartmill. She decided she'd fetch a sprig of the tree for the next show and tell, once the holiday break ended. She hoped it would still be blooming then.

The two girls walked side by side, the gap between them changing according to the pattern of the woods. Their steps were loud on the leaves, but they weren't really so loud.

They took another break. Lucinda Mae figured they weren't but a mile or so to the place. Again, they said little. Lucinda Mae felt a strong desire to tell Jean the story of how the one-eyed Santa lady lost her eyes, but she reminded herself that she could only tell it one time, to one person. She would wait. Maybe she'd tell Jean in a few years, maybe she'd wait even longer than that. As they rested, Jean shared a pack of M&Ms. Lucinda Mae listened to the sounds of their chewing until a strange whistle caught her attention.

"What the heck was that?" Jean said. Lucinda Mae hopped to her feet and gazed around the area. Jean did the same. There was a squirrel chasing another squirrel. Three big birds made a ruckus at the base of a grapevine tangle.

"There," Jean said, pointing up the slope.

"Where?" Lucinda Mae said.

The whistle, a human sound, blasted again. Lucinda Mae followed the noise to its origins. There was a man in hunting clothes at the base of a big poplar tree. He held an old-fashioned-looking gun over the crook of his arm, the kind with a hammer like she'd seen Mr. Hall shoot one time with her dad out back of the corral. She remembered how the gun had made a lot of smoke when fired.

"That's Coach," Jean said.

"Who?" Lucinda Mae asked. Irritation crawled under her skin.

Jean went on. "Coach Killigrew, from school. He's got a muzzleloader. He's a big hunter." Lucinda Mae felt a mix of comfort and annoyance. She liked knowing there was another person in the area, but she preferred the privacy of their mission too.

"Wait," she said to Jean. She had started walking. "Let's tell him we're just up gathering, um, looking for treasures to give for Christmas presents."

Jean gave her a funny expression, like understanding and confusion were having an argument on her face.

"No, let's tell him we're looking for a lost dog," Jean said after a thoughtful moment. "A beagle. It'll sound more believable. And it looks like Hoss has already found him," Jean said. They all stared at Coach. He was petting Hoss behind the ears where he stood by the tree up the slope.

"Okay, looking for a dog it is," Lucinda Mae said with some dismay in her voice. "A beagle. But since when did you start being so sneaky?"

The man placed his gun on the ground so that it aimed away from the girls as they approached. He bore a curious, friendly look on his bearded face. After a brief exchange, he said he hadn't seen any dogs except for Hoss. The girls said they hadn't seen any deer. Jean, who often had to say a little something extra, mentioned they'd crossed a lot of game paths, that there was a good bit of deer scat. This was true. The man said he had seen it, too, but it was about time for him to head back. He'd been hunting since early dawn. That was all, a brief visit. Lucinda Mae was relieved. She noticed with delight that Jean was proud to have been seen high on Painter Mountain on Christmas Eve by the man who coached Arlen's football team. She saw, too, that she probably wanted to tell the coach what they were really doing. She was glad that Jean didn't do that.

Another little while of walking and they arrived at the place with the boulders. There was still ice at the falls, but it had melted and more water ran than Lucinda Mae remembered. It sounded like someone taking a shower. The dead deer bore a riper stench now, too, and instead of one vulture, five had flapped to a roost upon Hoss' approach.

"Nasty," Jean said.

"Worse than it was," Lucinda Mae added.

"This place is wild," Jean went on.

"The cave's over here," Lucinda Mae said. She headed that direction but stopped after a couple of steps. She saw the gun and the knapsack exactly where she'd left them and felt great waves of relief run through her. She had been worried Coach might have discovered the gun, or some other hunter or explorer.

"Jean, what time do you have?"

"It's twelve-thirty," she said.

"We better get busy," Lucinda Mae said, looking over at the cave.

"Busy, yes, that's what I was thinking, too," said Jean with a grin. "We better get on it. Here you go, mop-head," she said as she handed her brother's flashlight to Lucinda Mae and then fetched her own. Jean offered her a bandana, too.

Lucinda Mae smiled back. She felt content. She wasn't without fear, but she felt deeply glad to be exactly where she was right then and there. "Okay," she said. "Okay, Jeanie Jeanie Bo Beanie."

"Merry Christmas Eve," Jean announced. She seemed to be speaking to the forest, the entire mountain, even the cave. "Here goes nothing."

Lucinda Mae shook her head and smiled. She was amused by her friend's sudden goofing, but she knew it was just a way to cover up the fear they felt about going back in the cave. She thought about her dad at the post office, helping the people with their mail. She saw her mother and Peanut. She saw them having lunch with Mimi, chatting about Christmases past, the baby, all sorts of stuff, the way they did. She wondered if they were worried about her and Jean.

"I'll go first," Lucinda said, sliding over the steep rim of the pit. Hoss whined fanatically just then.

"Shup," Jean said to the dog, offering him another fig bar and then eating it herself when he ignored the snack. Then she followed Lucinda Mae into the dark opening.

Their lights were on, beams flashing around in the dark. Lucinda Mae could smell the same greasy, rancid smell of burnt lard, but after a minute decided it was weaker than it had been the prior day.

She knelt. She had to kneel. To squat was not practical; she couldn't move that way. So she knelt and crawled. "Jean," she whispered.

"Here," she whispered back. Jean was right behind her.

They started to see remnants of the mining operations. Rotting chunks of lumber, rusted nails, odd bits of steel, broken glass. Lucinda Mae stopped.

She shone the light ahead, but so far the passage was full of curves, one after another, limiting the view. She rubbed at the walls of the cave. It felt like dirt and crumbled under her hand. She saw, rubbing again, that her fingernails were turning a stronger shade of blue. She craned her head around to see Jean, held up her hand for her friend. Jean checked her own hand and nodded. They knew better than to say anything out loud.

Lucinda Mae thought for a moment about turning back. Now and then she heard Jean's voice, whispering, and though she couldn't make out what she was saying, she could tell they were encouraging words. She crawled ahead, careful not to place her knees or hands on any of the broken glass or sharp metal. Jean followed.

Around the next curve, the passage widened. The girls knelt next to one another and progressed together. They were a good distance in there. Lucinda Mae scanned the ground with great care. She felt Miss Cartmill's presence.

Each time Lucinda Mae stopped, she listened hard. The smell had not changed, but there was no sound like voices or wind, nothing like the sounds they'd heard the last time.

Around the next curve, they came into a kind of opening. They could stand in the middle, and Lucinda Mae turned to see Jean, but she was facing a corner. She followed the beam of Jean's flashlight to a pile of bones and felt a shiver.

"It's varmint bones," Jean muttered quietly. "Don't worry."

"Raccoon?" whispered Lucinda Mae.

"Yes, and opossum, fox, rats, and stuff. Look at this," her friend said. Lucinda Mae saw where Jean's light now puddled against a pile of what must have been soapstone, all shapes and sizes. But then, too, she heard it. The voices. Jean shot her a glance, her light flooding Lucinda Mae's eyes. For a second, she couldn't see and then when she could see, she saw Jean scrambling at the pile, sweeping it into a pillow case. She was loading it fast. Lucinda Mae was stunned. Jean hadn't told her about bringing a pillowcase. What a smart thing to do. But now the voices grew louder.

"Come on," Lucinda Mae whispered as she scurried back in the direction they'd come. She felt terrified and elated. She'd heard the voices so clearly they could have been inside her ear. She looked back. She was relieved to see Jean not far behind her, scraping along fast, like a bear. She was coming. Her eyes were huge. She dragged the sack. The lard smell was so strong, and now it mixed with the smell of burning hair. Try as she might, Lucinda Mae could not hold her nose, could not just breathe through her mouth.

Lucinda Mae reached the edge of the pit, Jean right behind her. Hoss was yowling a sound like fear might sound if fear had a voice.

"Come on!" Jean said.

"The gun, the knapsack!" Lucinda Mae said as she grabbed them. Now Jean was already running down the hill, away from the mine, sack flung over her shoulder. Hoss followed.

Some big part of Lucinda Mae wanted to go back and see the owners of the voices in the cave, and then go on up to the corral. She thought of the voices in the cave, how strangely scary they were for not being particularly scary voices, just different, just odd. She thought of the reindeer antler, Miss Cartmill, Mr. Speed, Peanut, her Mimi, the hogs, her hens. She thought of squirrel meat thawing on the kitchen counter, and then she ran with the swiftness of all squirrels, or at least tried to imagine doing so.

They ran pretty much the same path as the prior day. They ran as fast as they could with their awkward loads, and as they ran Lucinda Mae's mind kept moving all over the place, and fast too, as if in time with the beating of her heart. She was disappointed, but she felt good to have the gun, the knapsack. She ducked suddenly under another low branch without slowing her stride. Her ankle felt good.

Ahead of her, Jean stopped. They were down the hill a mile or so from where they'd seen Coach. Lucinda Mae quit running too, and they stood there among the trees and shrubs. They looked at one another and then they looked back up the hill. Their breathing had plenty to say.

9

Jean was the first to speak. "I'm not sure what we were running from."

"The voices," Lucinda Mae said, downcast. She placed the gun on the ground and took off her knapsack. Hoss had curled in a tight ball in a nest of leaves. He appeared to want to disappear. As she stood up again, Lucinda Mae noticed that the day had turned cloudy but that the air still held warmth. It wasn't cooling as it normally did this time of day in winter. She felt a moist breeze blowing now out of the south.

"But what were they?" Jean asked, looking from her fingernails to her best friend. She spoke in a hushed voice. She sounded both defeated and curious. Her dirty, stuffed pillowcase lay like some kind of melted snowman in the leaves at her feet.

Lucinda Mae looked at Jean's fingernails, which like hers were a deep shade of sky blue, and then gazed back up the mountain. She shifted her vision through the winter trees. "Don't know. They won't come down here."

A crow zoomed above them. Maybe it was a hawk.

"Are we going back up?" Jean asked.

Lucinda Mae looked at Jean and felt like laughing and crying at the same time. She saw that deep down Jean wanted to go back up as much as she didn't want to go back up. And it had to be getting on three, if it wasn't three already. "It's late," she said.

"What about Miss Cartmill?" Jean said.

"I know," Lucinda Mae said. She saw Jean checking her watch.

"Just after three," Jean said. "Will be near dark in an hour or so."

"We better get on home," Lucinda Mae said. "We'll try again. We'll figure this out, find some antler. We'll help Miss Cartmill. We have to. No way we're giving up on her."

"Yes," Jean said. "We sure will. She needs us. Why don't you call on the walkie-talkie?" Jean suggested. "Tell your ma we're running a little late."

Lucinda Mae worked it out with her mother over the walkie-talkie. The exchange was brief, but everything was made clear. They had to rest but then they'd be down directly.

"Let's have a look in the pillowcase," Jean said. Lucinda Mae munched on a fig bar from the knapsack. All the excitement had made her hungry. As she ate, she thought over the last days. It had been, so far, a winter break like none other, and she noticed how things were happening in pairs. She and Jean had made two trips to Mr. Speed's house and then they'd made two trips up the mountain and into the cave, and twice, too, they'd hustled down the mountain. It seemed odd somehow, or maybe not odd enough. Maybe there needed to be a third trip to Mr. Speed's or a third trip up the mountain. Maybe all these things happening in twos added up to sticking to it, that if sometimes things didn't work out the first time, you had to try again, and then maybe you had to keep on trying.

Jean dumped the contents of the pillowcase on the cold, leafy ground. Lucinda Mae studied the pile of stones and grit. Bits of dry-rotted lumber and rusty metal and a shard of burlap were part of the mix. Mostly, it looked like soapstone. Lucinda Mae's eyes fell on a couple of the larger pieces. They were brick-sized. Hoss wandered over now and sniffed with great interest at the heap. While she marveled at how heavy a load Jean had carried, she had the sudden idea to make her father a

Christmas present of the soapstone. She'd heard it wasn't hard to carve.

"We better get on down the mountain," Lucinda Mae said.

"Coming down the mountain," Jean part said, part sung. Lucinda Mae looked at her funny. "It's from a song," Jean said, "a song my uncle likes. I'm going to pack these up again."

Lucinda Mae bent to help Jean load the pillowcase. "You mind if I take these two?" she asked.

Jean said, "I don't mind, but why?"

"Keepsakes," Lucinda Mae said.

"I want some too," said Jean.

"Of course," Lucinda Mae said as she put the big pieces of soapstone in the pockets of her orange vest. The vest was heavy with their weight but she didn't mind. It was all downhill from here.

๑ ๑

The friends hiked down to Painter Mountain's lowest flank in thoughtful silence. Hoss walked right with them—no rousting about for him. The sun was behind a thick blanket of cloud cover. They noticed lots of birds feeding on the ground, chickadees and other birds. It felt likely that Christmas morning would bring snow.

Mr. Hall had dropped off Lucinda Mae's dad and was just pulling across the plank bridge over the creek when they arrived from back of the corral. Hoss ran immediately to Mimi's place, which brought the woman to her porch. She shouted to them, but they couldn't make out what she said. They waved hello.

Lucinda Mae's dad stood at the door to the mud-room. He watched the girls approach with a look of relief and pride.

"How'd it go?" he asked.

"No squirrels," Lucinda Mae said. She'd noticed her dad looking at the gun, nodding.

"At least you tried," her father said as he took the .20 gauge from her tired arms. She figured he'd inspect it, but he held its barrel skyward, pointed away from everyone, and he looked at Jean.

"Howdy, Jean," he said. "Thanks for joining Cinda today."

"It was something," Jean said.

"What's in the sack?" Mr. Coggins asked.

"Stones we gathered," Jean added.

"That's a load," Mr. Coggins said. "And look at that. I see you like to paint your fingernails sky blue, too."

"I wanted yellow," Jean said with a goofy smile, "like Cinda's dresses."

He laughed. "Now come on in, grab a bite, sister blue-nails, you fluff-tail hunters. Lucinda Mae's mom made chocolate chip cookies, she's feeling much better, and we're getting to work on the Christmas tree soon, could use your help with little Peanut man."

"Yes, sir," Jean growled with appetite and scurried to the door.

Lucinda Mae smiled and followed, while Mr. Coggins went off to the wood stack to fetch a load.

⊷ ⊶

Lucinda Mae and Jean sat at the kitchen table, drinking milk with their cookies. Mrs. Coggins had used Christmas cookie cutters, so they bit into fir trees and reindeer and wreath-shapes. The warmth of the house made them feel sluggish and tired in a good, relieved way. Lucinda Mae felt many things as her dad passed on his way back outside after filling the woodbox by the stove. He carried a pail of ash. It was good to be home. It was also bittersweet. That they'd failed to find the reindeer antler settled like a stone in her mind. She felt sadness but also determination. She wanted to go look again. Miss Cartmill was always close to her thoughts, and she pictured her now. Her mom was feeling better—why not Miss Cartmill, too?

They moved to the living room. Lucinda Mae took Peanut from her mom. Now he hunkered in her arms against her chest. She sat on the floor, back against the couch where Jean sat, down at the other end. Christmas music played on the transistor radio, the usual songs, cheery and reverent. Now and then Jean stood and helped Mr. and Mrs. Coggins string the lights around the tall part of the tree. It was a fine tree. Lucinda Mae liked the smell of it as much as the size.

Her mom really was feeling stronger after her morning cold. Her voice was back to normal as she asked questions about their hunting adventure. Lucinda Mae answered carefully. She gave an affectionate glance to Jean that said, *Keep quiet.*

"You sound so tired, Cinda," her mom said. "I hope you're not getting sick."

Lucinda Mae suddenly felt exasperated. She wanted to tell her mom that she wasn't sick, that she was lying and she sounded sick when she was lying, but there was a woman who was sick, and she and Jean needed to help her, and needed to do it without grownups getting in the way. But she said nothing. Soon, her parents were talking amongst themselves about dinner, and Lucinda Mae tuned out. She sat in a dazed quiet.

"Girls," Mr. Coggins said then.

"Yes," Lucinda Mae said.

"Why don't you go down to Speed's place," her dad started, "and invite him for Christmas Eve dinner."

"What?" Lucinda Mae asked as she stole a glance at Jean, who looked like she'd just seen a ghost. This, this was a total surprise. She studied her mom's face and then her dad's. They both appeared casual but there was a twinkle in their eyes that Lucinda Mae didn't know how to read. She felt like they were smiling, not just on their faces; it seemed like their whole bodies were smiling.

"Yes," Mrs. Coggins said. "Your dad and I were talking it over. We hate to think of him being alone like he always is. Please, go on, invite him for dinner."

"Are you sure?" Lucinda Mae asked. She looked at Jean, then. Jean was looking at her like *what the heck is going on.*

"He loves squirrel," Mrs. Coggins said. "It'll be interesting. He knows things."

"Go on," Mr. Coggins said. And then he added, looking at Jean, "You Underwoods are welcome as well. Tell your parents to bring the whole crew."

"We're headed to my grandparent's house at seven," Jean said. She sounded disappointed. "Uncle Larry's feeling better and bringing his family. He always plays Christmas music on his mandolin. But thank you."

"Mom," Lucinda Mae said as she handed her the Peanut man, who was still smiling at the tree. "Should I whip up the drop biscuits for the pot pie?"

"I did that already," her mama said. "But thanks for remembering and for grinding the flour. And thanks for checking in on the walkie-talkie." She paused a minute, but everyone could tell she had more to say. "And what about Miss Cartmill? I haven't been able to stop thinking about her. I saw her at the grocery today. She looked . . . I don't know. Always alone, too. Times I've seen her, I figured she had some problem with eating, trying to keep from getting fat and getting too skinny. But it's not that, I don't think now." She paused again, thinking. "If Speed comes tonight, I'll ask him."

Lucinda Mae sat there, trying to breathe easy, but the waves kept coming, waves of suspicion, guilt, wonder, confusion, curiosity, joy. She saw that Jean was also barely containing a lot of feels. Did her parents know? Did Mr. Speed tell them about how they'd come in his house, about the reindeer antler, the stolen map? Maybe they figured it out. Or maybe Mimi had put it together. Or Miss Cartmill. Good gracious.

Before they started for Mr. Speed's place, Jean stood by while Lucinda Mae fed her hens.

"There's something funny going on," Jean said.

"That's the truth," said Lucinda Mae as she counted the eggs. There were only eight today, which made the girl think of those paw prints she'd seen. Her hens often shied from laying well after they'd been scared in some way. "It's too funny to think about too much," she added.

"I guess," Jean said, "but I can't stop thinking about it. I wish I could join for dinner, though. You have to tell me everything. Remember everything and tell me how it goes, every little bit, okay?"

"Of course," Lucinda Mae said with a smile as she turned to take the eggs inside.

She laid the egg basket on the table and paused. She thought about asking her parents what they knew but decided against it. If they wanted her to know, they'd tell her. She ran to the living room and gave them each a hug.

"See you in a while," she shouted to her folks as she headed out the door.

❧ ❧

The air was heavy as they walked to Speed's. They crossed the plank bridge and took the road. Evening light lay creamy over the land. Lucinda Mae watched Jean bear the weight of the soapstone, the pillowcase slung over her shoulder. Beyond the sound of their boots on the gravel, the creek ran, and she listened until it could have been the sound of her own breathing.

Jean wore an expectant look on her face as they waited at Speed's door. Lucinda Mae wondered if she was nervous, like she was herself, and if she thought, too, that Mr. Speed had told her parents that the girls might be exploring Painter Mountain—maybe that they had snooped around his house without his permission.

"Good evening," the old man said as he opened the door.

"Mr. Speed, happy Christmas eve," said Jean.

"You're back," he said.

"Yes," Lucinda Mae said.

"What's that load on your shoulder?" Speed asked Jean.

"Soapstone," Jean answered.

"Bring it in then," Mr. Speed said, his face lighting up. "And don't tell me where you got it." He stepped aside to make room. Lucinda Mae thought she saw a smirk on his face, a knowing smirk. The house was warm. He had been working, making medicines, Lucinda Mae could tell by the aroma. There was steam in the air. "Feels like snow," Speed said as he closed the door.

"It does," said Lucinda Mae. She studied his face.

They pulled up chairs around the fire. Jean fetched wood from the back porch. Lucinda Mae felt a little strange with the quiet. "What's new, Mr. Speed?" she asked but as soon she asked it, she felt silly.

He looked at her a moment. His face was kind and then it turned a shade toward serious. "I saw painter tracks this morning," he said, "clear as day."

Jean was back in the room now. "Painter tracks," Jean said, her voice anxious and curious both. Lucinda Mae knew that Jean took a special interest in wild animals, often read up on them in books.

"It's been a while since I saw painter tracks," Mr. Speed said. "But I'm fairly certain."

"When did you see one last?" Jean asked.

"Been twenty years or so," Speed answered. "Though I doubt they disappeared entirely. They're some secretive, smart animals."

"Wow," said Jean.

"Have to say I'm pleased to see one coming around," Speed went on. He looked at Jean with knowing eyes. He sipped from his mug again and then looked to Lucinda Mae in a warm, interested way. "I'm curious about your sack of soapstone," he said. "You must have gone in an old mine cave, must have, to be bearing soapstone."

"We did go in," she said, and ran her hands along her yellow corduroy dress at the thighs. She wondered why she wasn't more nervous about telling him this, and decided that she trusted the man, and that he trusted her. She saw Mr. Speed's eyes go to her fingernails.

"I see that you did go in," he said then, nodding at her nails. Jean held up her hands now, followed by Lucinda Mae. Speed studied them. "Both of you."

"That's right," Jean said. "And you should have seen us two come scrambling out of there. It was like our tails were on fire."

Lucinda Mae couldn't believe what her friend had just said. She tried to glare at Jean but it wouldn't come. This was confusing. She realized she felt grateful and also a little heavy, grateful that it wasn't a secret, their adventure, but also like she'd lost something, something that had just belonged to her and Jean. The fact that they'd not found the antler felt newly bothersome, too. An ache started behind her eyes as she thought about Miss Cartmill. At least they'd tried, she reminded herself.

"Mossies," Speed muttered.

"Mossies?" the girls asked, nearly in unison. The fire crackled. The room was warm.

"Creepy sound, and we smelled them, too," Jean added.

"I believe it," Speed muttered. "And I believe I warned you girls about venturing up that mountain alone."

"It had to be done. For Miss Cartmill." Lucinda Mae paused to hold back the tears she felt rising, and then she went on, weakly, "I wish we'd found some, though."

Mr Speed looked at them with great care and concern. He looked proud of them. Lucinda Mae smiled to see that look on his face, and Mr. Speed and Jean smiled as well. "You're brave girls. Saucy, too, to take the map from my notebook." Lucinda Mae felt a sudden lead weight in her chest.

"We can give that back to you," Jean said. She looked from Speed to Lucinda Mae.

"Yes, I will," Lucinda Mae said. Her voice felt crisp, clear, and she went on, "That was me who did that, not Jean."

"That's okay, you keep it," Mr. Speed said. "Just pass it on, when the time's right, pass it on to someone else who might need it."

"That we will. Thank you, Mr. Speed," Lucinda Mae said.

"What is it that turns the nails sky blue?" Jean asked. "Mossies?"

Mr. Speed hunched in thought. His eyes narrowed as he examined again the girls' hands. After a minute, he responded. "Must have been the mossies, that smell. And those fingernails. If I remember right, it fades."

"They do fade!" Lucinda Mae said.

"Mossies, the old timers call them," Speed began. "Some say they're part opossum and part human. Others say they don't exist at all, that it's just wind from deep in the cave. You don't hear about them much since the mining stopped."

Lucinda Mae thought of that word she saw on the page with saucy in her Mimi's dictionary, "satyr." It had something to do with mixed creature life. She couldn't remember. "It sounded like voices, Mr. Speed," she said. "Not like any wind I ever heard. Have you been in that cave? There's a waterfall near it."

"Yes, a long while back," he said, "and my guess is there's some mineral in the soil in that cave, something stirred up by the mining. It gets in your blood through your skin. Hard telling, though."

"You mean it's not magic?" Jean said quickly.

"It's magic," the old man answered, "a sort of magic."

"What about the mossies and the one-eyed Santa lady in a red dress, the carriage, reindeer and other animals, isn't that all magic?" Jean asked.

"It's what you want it to be," he said, matter of fact. "The magic comes when you believe it, when you see the real world down deep, not just on the surface. And you don't shy away from it. Doctors and drugstores offer good medicines, but you know that many of those remedies come from plants. And you don't always have to go to the drugstore for medicine. And not for blue nail polish either, it seems." He smiled now. You could hear him grinning as he continued. "Drugstores haven't been around forever. And these hills, what they call the Gorges, they got all kinds of magic down deep in the roots and rocks and soil. It's no wonder one-eyed Santa or whoever that was landed here way back that warm Christmas and diversified her team. These hills ought to be called the healing hills. It seems people are mighty quick to call things scary, and places, even other people. They call them scary when they don't understand them. I have a hunch you kids thought I was scary or strange, maybe was why you were spying on me, rooting around in my house on the sly."

Lucinda Mae looked at Jean. She looked around the room. She sort of grinned and sort of didn't grin, like she was embarrassed and like she had just eaten a good meal, too.

"Mr. Speed," Lucinda Mae said after a little while. "We'd like to have you for Christmas Eve dinner tonight."

"Oh," he said.

"My Mimi and my Aunt Janet and me and my parents and baby brother. Squirrel pot pie for dinner, other good stuff too."

"Why, that sounds nice," he said. "I'd like that."

"Well," Lucinda Mae said, "we'd like that, too." She saw the night was bearing down heavy out the window. There was a coppery glow to the twilight.

"Let's have a look in that bag," Speed said.

Jean reached for it but paused. "Dump it on the floor?"

"Sure," Speed said.

Jean emptied the pillowcase. The soapstone made a commotion as it tumbled out on the old wood boards.

"I haven't seen that much soapstone in a good while," Speed said in wonder as he bent over to fetch a few pieces. The girls followed suit. Each held the soapstone and looked at it and then at Speed. "Mighty fine stuff," he said. "And lots of it." He looked at the fire then. Lucinda Mae watched him. He looked like he was remembering the old days. She looked in the fire as well, to see if it might tell her what he was seeing. After a while, Lucinda Mae saw that the old man was studying the pile again. He reached for a piece of rock that had a slightly different texture than the others. It was narrower, with little bumps, and a slightly more polished sheen. "Mind if I keep this one?" he asked. Lucinda Mae and Jean looked at one another.

Something had changed in the room. The twilight was turning from copper to peach.

"Of course," Lucinda Mae said. Jean nodded in support and then stood.

"Well," Jean said. She was looking at his watch. "I need to get home."

"I better do the same," Lucinda Mae said as she stood. Mr. Speed stayed in his chair. He stared at the stone in his hand, a strange, thoughtful look on his face.

"I'll be down in a while," Mr. Speed said after a minute. Lucinda Mae sensed a freshening in his voice. "That I will. I do like some squirrel pot pie."

Jean Underwood went up the road and Lucinda Mae headed the other direction. They made plans to get together the next day, on Christmas afternoon. Lucinda Mae, on the way home, stopped at one of her favorite places by Painter Creek for a spell. She watched the water and the rocks as twilight's last glow slowly faded. She squatted at the bank. She felt tired but good. As she let the cold liquid move through her hands, against and around her fading blue fingernails, she glanced downstream. There wasn't enough light to see clearly, but she thought she saw something on the opposite bank, about a bus-length down the creek. It was a creaturely shape she saw, she thought, and pretty large, like a big dog, but it was more cat-like in shape. She tried to look closer but things were blurry. The dark was too thick. It must have been a trick of the eyes, she thought, but then she felt a shiver run all through her. She hurried home.

Once in the house, Lucinda Mae took a long, warm shower and then dressed in one of her fancier yellow dresses for Christmas Eve. A velour one with raised stitching over the chest. She admired its softness and color. It made her remember the witch hazel flower. It made her smile. She felt good, glanced at the two chunks of stone on her desk from Jean's pillowcase, and then headed into the rest of the house. There were a lot of voices.

When she entered the kitchen, she couldn't believe her eyes. There was Miss Cartmill. Miss Cartmill. She was holding Peanut in her thin right arm and eating with her other hand a cracker with a slice of venison bologna. She wore a beautiful green wool skirt and a red turtleneck sweater.

"Hello," said her teacher.

Lucinda Mae tried to speak but nothing came out. She was smiling so big she felt her jaw straining. So many feelings were running through her. "Hi," she said eventually. Peanut grew alert at the sound of his sister's voice. Lucinda Mae kissed him on the cheek and stepped back, still in shock to be seeing her teacher. She noticed Mr. Speed now. He wore a pretty blue shirt buttoned up all the way to his throat, a vest of leather—it looked homemade—over that.

"Deerskin," he said, having followed her eyes. "I brought a friend. I hope you don't mind."

"No, sir," said the girl, "I don't mind at all."

"You're a saucy one, old man," came her Mimi's voice from the doorway to the living room. She sounded feisty tonight. "Get your hobbly leg in here and help me hang some ornaments on this tree." Lucinda Mae could smell the rich, peppery smell of the dinner cooking. She saw headlights out the window as her Aunt Janet arrived. Her mother and father were in with Mimi. Somebody turned on the radio. "O Little Town of Bethlehem" came through the air. Chills rose all over her skin, chills of happiness and mystery, nourishing chills.

"Lucinda Mae," her teacher said. "I appreciate everything you've done for me."

The girl felt a smile come to her face. It was a powerful smile, from a place of deep and startled surprise. "Um, we tried. I wish we'd done better. But we'll try again," she said.

"Mr. Speed told me everything. You've done plenty," Miss Cartmill said just as they were called to the dinner table.

❧ ❧

Lucinda Mae didn't say too much while they ate. She felt confused but also happy to see that her parents were enjoying the company. Now and then she stole glances at Miss Cartmill and saw a thin, serious woman who was enjoying the company and the talk and the food. Lucinda Mae looked at the tree from Linklet's; it sparkled with ornaments and lights as if it was part of the meal.

When the plates were nearly cleared, Mr. Speed asked how far into the cave she and Jean had found the soapstone.

"Wait!" Lucinda Mae's dad started. "You girls went in a cave?"

"Yes," Lucinda Mae said as she watched her parents looking at each other with concern. "Twice we went in; it is an old soapstone mine."

"Lucinda Mae and Jean are something courageous," Mr. Speed said. "Must be that Painter Mountain water they've been drinking," he added with a big smile.

Lucinda Mae saw that her parents were settling down. They didn't look mad. They looked proud and also a little confused. So she decided to explain. She explained with care and detail about her and Jean's adventures on Painter Mountain. She saw everyone listening with equal care. There was a quiet when she finished. Then Mr. Speed asked her if they'd seen rusted old bed parts under an overhanging boulder near the falls. She told him yes. At that, Mr. Speed explained how the cot under the boulder marked the place where two brothers hid out during the Civil War. The cot came later, he said, as a hunter had left it there. One brother had been living in Pennsylvania, working as a carpenter's apprentice, and he had been called to fight for the Union. The other had been called from the farm here in Painter Hollow to fight for the Confederacy. They weren't much for fighting, and they both, unknown to the other, snuck off for home, became deserters. It was a dangerous thing to do. Men roamed the countryside, hunting to arrest deserters, or do worse. It was the brother from Pennsylvania who made it to Painter Mountain first. He holed up in that outcrop, and was making out okay, scratching a living off the land, when his Confederate brother showed up one day, with a bad bayonet wound on his leg. The men helped each other through a long winter, sneaking down real careful to the farms around Laurel Fork to help out in exchange for supplies now and then.

So much in the past week had been fitting together that Lucinda Mae should not have been surprised when Mr. Speed said the brothers were Cartmills, distant relatives of his and of Miss Cartmill, and that the one who'd been in Pennsylvania was Miss Cartmill's great-great-grandfather, and that her teacher was living and teaching in Laurel Fork in order not just to teach, a job she loved and believed in, but also to research her family's history for a book she was writing about them. Miss Cartmill nodded her head then. It was a slight movement, as though her neck hardly worked to accomplish the nod.

Lucinda Mae thought about what she heard. It was a lot. Under the table, she ran her hands over the soft velour of her dress. It was almost hard to believe, all these connections. It was a lot of things coming together, and it made her feel—she wasn't quite sure what. Lucky. And full. Like if you paid attention to it, all life had a kind of pattern, like the marks of a hard freeze on a window, a leaf's veins, the path of water through the stones on Painter Creek. She suspected, too, that no matter how hard you paid attention, you'd never see the whole pattern, that it was changing all the time, though maybe you could feel it, the changing or the pattern or both.

⊰ ⊱

Later in the night, after the group had sung carols around the tree and people were mingling, Lucinda Mae noticed a thermos that she'd seen in Mr. Speed's kitchen. She spied Miss Cartmill then pouring herself a mug of whatever was in it. Mr. Speed approached the girl, as though he'd been watching her.

She looked at him, saw the grateful smile on his face. Then his face turned serious as he looked from Lucinda Mae to Miss Cartmill, nodding as the teacher sipped from the mug.

"That wasn't a piece of soapstone, that chunk I kept from Jean's pillowcase," he said. He started on by, headed to the kitchen for some ice cream, but Lucinda

Mae stopped him. She'd heard what he'd said, but it had taken a minute for the meaning to move all through her mind.

"What was it?" she asked. A chunk of bone or maybe something the mossies had left?

Mr. Speed stopped and turned, looked her hard and kindly in the eye, as if through her eyes and into her memories of the last few days. "Chunk of reindeer antler," he said. "And a chunk right gnawed on by those mossies or squirrels or something. But there was enough antler to brew that tea your teacher's sipping now. Enough for another several pots."

Lucinda Mae didn't know what to say. The word "gnawed" kept ringing in her ears. She wondered if she'd heard Mr. Speed correctly. "Did you say it was a chunk of reindeer antler?" she asked him.

"Yes. I'm sorry I didn't tell you earlier," Mr. Speed said. Lucinda Mae felt a smile stretching her cheeks. "I wasn't sure," Mr. Speed went on. "I wanted Miss Cartmill to sip on it a while first. It does something strange, reindeer-antler tea. It makes your toes tingle a little while after you start sipping on it. Sure enough, Miss Cartmill felt that in her toes, just right as dinner was being served. That's how we finally knew. Let's just hope it can help. I mean, it's already helped her though, just knowing how much you and Jean love her, how you were willing to do all that you did."

Lucinda Mae felt a great commotion in her heart. "I need to call Jean and tell her," she said. She felt herself giggling as tears welled up behind her eyes. She stared at the mug at Miss Cartmill's thin lips. "An accident," Lucinda Mae said, feeling a joyful tear running down her cheek. "Funny that it'd turn up that way."

"There are other words for it, Miss Mae, besides accident. Lots of ways to look at it. The main thing is there was an old chunk of reindeer antler. And Miss Cartmill's sipping a brew of it. Now, you'll have to excuse me," Mr. Speed said. "Your Mimi's invited me to her place for a game of checkers."

Lucinda Mae wasn't sad. These weren't tears of grief. She felt something different. It wasn't like any feeling she'd known. Or it was like all the feelings she'd known, all at once and all the time, a swarming tenderness.

Now Lucinda Mae started full on laughing. She couldn't stop laughing. Big tears rose and ran down her cheek as she giggled. Her red hair bounced along with her head and shoulders, her whole body, as she laughed. "You be careful, Mr. Speed," she said with a snort. "My Mimi's a tough one when it comes to checkers."

"I'll do that," he said with a chuckle as he hobbled to the door at the mudroom, cane tapping. "Now you have a merry Christmas."

"I already am," Lucinda Mae said. "You, too."

Lucinda Mae was exhausted when she laid down for bed, but try as she might, she couldn't sleep. She kept hearing Jean's amazed, excited voice on the telephone as she'd told her the news of the antler, Mr. Speed, Miss Cartmill, the brothers by the waterfall, all the relations. Eventually, she abandoned her yellow pillow and sat at her desk, studying the two chunks of soapstone from Jean's pillowcase, running them around in her hands. To feel the smooth surface another way, she held one of the stones against her cheek. She yawned a few times but still didn't feel like sleeping. Her hair, when she touched it, felt like a mess.

It was then, over the corner of the larger stone, that she saw her old pocket knife where she kept it on the desk. She took it in her hand and opened the blade. She fiddled around with the knife's edge against the stone. It was surprising how easily the rock could be worked.

The moon was behind the clouds. Snow was falling, a wet, big-flaked snow, like a swarm of moths. But in the wee hours of dark, as Lucinda Mae still played with stone and knife, the moon peeked through a break in the clouds. It was that time when the moon, waning but still big, stays in the sky a good part of the morning like it's lost. Lucinda Mae yawned, her fingernails still blue but starting to fade. She had been sculpting the stones for hours. Dawn was near. She had put aside one of the stones and was running out of steam working on the other, which bore a similar pattern as the first. She stopped, closed the knife, and regarded the shapes.

She had been pressuring the knife blade along the stone according to where it was most willing to be worked. She'd scratched and carved and poked with no set idea, as if the stone was pretty enough that she trusted a pleasing shape would emerge. The stones were no longer raw and brick-like except at the bases on which they stood, firm and heavy, on her desk. Each piece was flat on the inside, and heavy enough to make a good bookend for her father and mother, a gift for Christmas. Her parents had many old books. They liked to read, when they had time.

Everything above the bases on the two pieces of soapstone flowed together in a way that felt very familiar. Lucinda Mae sat there, a bit hunched over in her yellow nightgown. She felt wondrous tired. Pale dust and chips of stone speckled her hair like snow. Her eyes were heavy, and she rubbed them with her chalky fingers and then she studied the soapstone to make sure she was seeing correctly. She started laughing through her nose at first and then through her mouth, a quiet laughter that came from way down deep. There was no doubt, no mistaking the pattern, the shape. She had made soapstone sculptures of reindeer antler. They had their rough spots, but Lucinda Mae saw it. She shook her head like this was the darnedest thing and looked more closely. Yes, and in each bookend, carved at the base of the antler, there was one single eye. One eye looking out, Lucinda Mae sensed, for what is true.

CPSIA information can be obtained
at www.ICGtesting.com
Printed in the USA
JSHW080244230223
38109JS00004B/16

9 781950 584048